To Debst Po''   14/8/12

Thanks

reading,

the reclusives

pubbing, and being
a great friend
to a great
friend, Matty.
Look after him.

mark damon puckett

ONION SCRIBE

PUBLISHING

"The Edible Harmonica" appeared first in *The Tusculum Review*, vol. 2, 2006.

Onion Scribe Publishing

Cover & Interior Design by Scribe Freelance | www.scribefreelance.com

Cover photograph and manipulation by Bill Havranek

ISBN: 978-0-9835435-0-3

www.markdamonpuckett.com

Published in the United States of America

CONTENTS

For Bret Easton Ellis

"But where's the lost young man?"
—A.E. Housman

I AM NOT A LANDSCAPER

Johann was now an academic who knew that he had been hired over more qualified people. His novel, *Razors in the Hair Nets*, had done very well in Mexico where he was pretty sure no people had read it, even if they had bought a lot of copies. Somehow, it sold a lot in Texas too. El Paso for some reason?! Essentially, it was about his time as a fast-food manager in Laredo while also taking care of his parents in a one-bedroom apartment and gradually moving further north with more hard work, better jobs. El Norte crapola (for the man) is what it was.

What made the book funny was that Johann was an alcoholic and yelled at his customers, but no one would fire him. In fact, the book was really about his attempts to *get* fired. He often laced strawberry shakes with tequila. He didn't care. Then he wrote his book and sent it to a publisher in Mexico who thought it was hilarious. Great, Johann thought, my alcoholism is funny. People are messed up, yo.

Well, anyway, now he was at a small university, a college maybe, he couldn't remember, and he had been sitting in his office all through the night trying to figure out how he got there. He was drinking a lot more these days and had no idea how to teach creative writing. After his first workshop yesterday afternoon, he had asked a slim, vivacious redhead (always stretching her back and pushing out her breasts) if she "wann' to be my girlfriend". While the girl was flattered, she immediately told the head of the department and he had been reprimanded.

During the whole workshop, students kept asking for a syllabus. "What's a syllabus?" he thought but made sure not to say. Now, in the middle of the night, he was looking it up in his office and still didn't understand what it meant because he couldn't even find it in the dictionary. At first he thought they were asking for the "silly bus".

Thank God Johann had learned to keep his mouth shut when he didn't understand something. Since he had a published book, people just assumed that his silence was some form of taciturn brilliance. That's right, cabrón! I know what taciturn means, which was by luck because he had just turned to it when he was trying to look up "syllabus".

The dictionary wasn't helping so he cracked open a warm Tecate and shotgunned it. His parents were doing better now that he had given them most of his book advance for a place of their own. He had a nice faculty apartment on campus for himself and was the visiting writer for the year. During the interview, they seemed to be thrilled that he was Mexican, given that the whole selection committee was white and female. He had learned that most universities used to be white and male. Now they were white and female and filled with minorities and gay people. What he wondered was how much of his position was the result of his book success and how much due to his ethnicity.

Luckily, he was able to get through the first workshop by giving his background, talking about his book and referring to his favorite writers. Weirdly enough, most of the people in the workshop were . . . white and female! The redhead had a body shape that defied reason. She was extremely pretty with a raspy, sexy voice that made everyone listen. She was tall with very long, slender legs. Normally, on such a lithe body she would have had smaller, perkier breasts. But no. This one had double d's or maybe even bigger. Whatever was after d's. E's? She just kept smiling at him. He assumed that she wanted to have sex, which is why it was so surprising to be rejected. Anyway, he had learned that it was illegal to date his students. This was a bummer because he liked tall redheads with large breasts.

His office was pretty cool. Not too big. Intimate. He had finished a six-pack and decided to pin up the Tecate case on the wall for decoration. It added red, yellow and white to the dull gray walls. He leaned back, kicked up his feet on his desk and took a nap. He had been living in what he thought *was* his apartment, at first, until he realized that no one else slept in their offices. The department head then informed him that he also had a small one-bedroom on campus.

To be honest, he preferred the office. As he dozed at his desk he dreamed of Mexico and the mountains and quiet local trains where people hopped on and sold peanuts during stops. One man in his village had no legs and would crawl down the aisles on with an accordion and play.

He did not belong here now, but he was here. He wanted to hide. From everyone. From his low-class past. From his not knowing English like he should. And mostly from his ignorance about teaching. Thankfully he could write. That was something, he supposed.

The chair where he was sleeping had been left by the last professor, a man who taught until he was 107 or something and who had brought in his three poodles, so that the chair now smelled of three, maybe even five poodles (that particularly rancid poodle smell that other dogs didn't seem to have). It was a curly, oily smell.

It occurred to him that he should write another book. He had been to a few bookstores and checked out what was considered literary, what was commercial. His book had been, basically, a reality t.v. show but a book. If he planned to get another job after this one, he needed to publish again. The college had even given him a brand new computer. Why not use it? He finished his half-nap and sat in front of the beaming white screen. Then he decided to write about ventriloquism, one of his favorite things.

When he was a poor kid, he used to receive toys from the Salvation Army. One such "toy" was a black doll with a curly afro named Lester. On the back of its head was a string that you pulled to open and close the mouth. It came with a book on ventriloquism, how to say "b" by keeping your mouth shut and really saying "d". He practiced with his doll and soon became a fixture in many of the local cafés. What he didn't realize was that people came to gawk at him, not to see his secondary linguistic skills. A small Mexican boy with a black doll was a strange sight indeed. However, it might be perfect for those white New York literary critics like Eli Lovelace who loved the fact that he was Mexican, almost to the point of forgetting his name. There was one Japanese critic, or maybe she was an Eskimo, who had liked his book but said it was "a quasi-cultural non-simile for immigration antagonism". He wasn't sure if this was good or bad.

He may have not known what a syllabus was, but he was coming to understand publishing better. With his ethnic background and with this current story about an odd Mexican boy being castigated for his love of his black ventriloquist doll, he had the racial element covered. He just had to write the book. The white computer screen beamed at him like a too-bright smile on a stupid actor, then he began to write, the black font of the letters and words filling up the white space and dimming it, like a dark cloud covering the sun:

"Pepe was a sweet boy [MAKE SURE HE IS NOT THE GAY, JUST SENSITIVE] from La Pesca, Mexico, who loved dolls, but when he received a ventriloquist doll from the Salvation Army, his life changed forever."

Johann took a break. The first sentence was a lot of work, or, moreover, a lot of work went into that first sentence, up to the point of writing. He was exhausted. As he guzzled his beer from the can, he opened his door and peeked out to see if there were any hot girls. Of course, it was like 5 a.m., so it was unlikely.

The university or college or whatever the hell it was, wasn't very nice, sort of like a prison's adopted brother. And he still had trouble saying *Wisconsin*. It kept coming out *Weesconsin*. On the morning of his first day, he had actually seen a girl walking a duck on a leash. Then when he looked closer, there was a leash around the girl's neck and she was being pulled along by another girl! Beloit was a strange place with strange people doing strange things.

He decided to make use of the free yellow sticky notes and create a list of things on his mind:

1) Figure out what a "syllabus" is
2) Figure out if this is a college or a university
3) Buy a soccer ball
4) Stop sleeping in office
5) Write new novel to keep from having to work in fast food
6) Get the poodle smells out of chair
7) Buy ventriloquist doll for research purposes

He was pretty sure that he had his workshop to teach only once a week. That meant he would not have to teach until next week. It was hard to keep track of the days when he drank so much. After a while he stopped worrying about it. He didn't feel like writing or being outside, and he wasn't exactly tired, but he wasn't bored either, just stuck in that non-place where you just feel by yourself with no friends, insignificant seeming, unable to go this way or that, yet simultaneously comfortable, buried up to your head.

When the café opened a few hours later, he bought a huge breakfast. Coffee. Sausage and egg sandwich. Banana. Orange juice in a carton that looked like a house. Oatmeal with pieces of frozen pineapple. He ate by himself and looked around furtively, thinking that Americans were cold and distant. El Norte, whatever. Then he realized there was almost no one in the cafeteria. Eating alone had to be the loneliest thing you could do. The chewing took longer and you had to listen to your teeth mashing instead of having the nice distraction of a friend. Wisconsin didn't have a lot of Mexican people.

As he ate, he wondered where he could buy another Lester doll. Recently, he had discovered this computer phenomenon known as the Enternet. On the Enternet you could buy anything you wanted. So maybe he would try that. He even had a credit card now. He liked the Enternet. One time, he bought twelve cases of Tecate (well, he did this more than once).

Suddenly, two students approached him and said hello, a young guy with hair the color of spinach and an odd girl who had three safety pins through her nose.

The girl spoke: "We were, liiiiike, wondering if you had the syllabus yet?"

"Soon, soon," he replied. "Next class."

"Great!"

If he could only remember when the next class was!

He chewed his bland gringo food and finished his breakfast. *This* was success? Where were the cheering crowds, the readers hungry for autographs, the nubile nymphs in his bed every night, the limos, the famous author friends? He hated to be alone. Even walking by himself back to the office across the quad was an exercise in humility. He was short and squat and everyone probably thought he was a landscaper. For a moment he considered buying a leaf blower and carrying it around the campus and aiming it at the hair of students as if it were a big blow dryer. Maybe he should write about a superhero landscaper with a fantastically heroic leaf blower that could blow away criminals into the air. The Mexican Tornado.

Why the hell did all these Mexicans have those noisy things strapped to themselves anyway? Even when he had arrived on campus, a group of five had approached him and handed him one. Never asked him anything. Just gave him a leaf blower and expected him to start blowing some leaves, except the five of them weren't blowing leaves at all because there were no leaves, just dust. They were blowing dust around, sometimes right into each other. When he told them he was a professor, they all looked at him like he was about to cut off their heads and roll them down a slide for the rain gods. Now he wanted that leaf blower back. It could have come in handy as a secret weapon for The Mexican Tornado.

As he entered the Humanities building and walked down the hallway, he began to feel irritated by anybody passing him. He muttered under his breath that he would kill them. Of course he was joking. He was not staggering, but he could feel all the beer he had been drinking through the night. And he just couldn't remember where his campus apartment was located. Wisconsin. My god, I'm in Wisconsin! He needed another nap. How was he going to figure out the next class? Maybe it was on the Enternet.

Back in his office, he called his parents and they seemed to be enjoying this new little city, although his father missed Mexico and had told him that books were written "mostly by homosexuals". Johann never really liked his dad. He was a narrow-minded bigot who looked and acted like Hitler. "The Mexican Hitler" was a short story idea, but he would wait until Papi died.

After he hung up the phone, he was hit with this homesickness for Mexico. It was simple, yes, and nothing happened and the people were sheep, but he loved it and he missed the countryside and the small town and salt air of La Pesca. He remembered the schoolchildren having an Easter parade down the main dirt road and pigs snorkeling around for the banana peels that boys and girls dropped from their one school bus.

He tried to type some more on his new book, but he was crippled with lethargy in that moment, so he fell asleep in the poodle-stinky chair and slept the sleep of someone who has just moved a long distance into a temporary home, the slumber of a stranger who is tired of being lonely but forced to be so beyond anything he can do.

■ ■ ■

He was not sure when he awoke, what time, but it was dark outside and he realized that he must have slept at least twelve hours. His breakfast had been early, maybe 8 a.m. Looking at the computer monitor, he noticed the corner said it was 11:33 p.m.

Fifteen hours!

But he felt so much better, not irritable as he had been when he wanted to kill people passing him in the hallway. It was a cozy spot for sure and he could see why white people hid out here. After he stood and stretched a bit, he opened his door.

It was deadly silent.

He closed the heavy door again.

Then he opened it again.

Nice door.

He had this whole building to himself, all this space to think. Maybe that was a problem; he didn't like to think too much.

Popping open another Tecate, he sat back with his ventriloquist story at his computer and thought that the writing life was pretty pathetic, just a sad excuse to be alone and away from everyone. Any words he tried to write felt false and so he went back to the chair and just drank, dozing here and there. He had gone through about five beers and maybe an hour had passed when he heard a thumping noise followed by some running and laughing. Thinking maybe he was drunk and dreaming, which he was, drunk, not dreaming, he dismissed it initially. He heard it again, though, and crept to the door. He ventured to open it slowly and when he stuck his head into the hallway, he was nearly decapitated by two gleeful students sprinting past him.

"Whoa!" one said to the other, slowing to a walk.

"I think I nearly took out a janitor!"

"Hey," Johann half-yelled.

The two young men stopped and walked back to him, not in hostility but curiosity. They could only be described as elfin, as they were both shorter than he and quite slim, each with wild blond hair that cascaded around their heads like wheat blowing in a hurricane.

"Wha'are you doing?" Johann slurred.

"Sorry, bro, is this the janitor's lounge?"

"Do you janit here?"

"Janit?"

"Yeah, janitor stuff?" The kid was serious.

"No, I'm professor."

The two looked at each other. "We've never seen you before," one said for both. He appeared to do all the talking.

"I just got here. Today was my first day."

"Gosh. We're here most nights."

"Yeah, what are you doing running up and down the halls?"

"Oh, it's l.a.r.p.ing."

"Larping?"

"Yeah. Live. Action. Role. Playing." He poked his finger at the air with each word.

"What's that?"

"Oh, it's just kind of fun. We dress up and hide and hit each other in the head with large styrofoam hammers and stuff like that. Haaaa. Hahaa!"

"Hah," Johann said, not knowing what to say. "You two related?"

"Yeah, brothers."

"Okay, sorry, I had just heard a noise and wanted to see what it was."

"We're not bothering you, are we?"

"No, no."

"Hey, can we have a beer?"

Johann looked at the Tecate in his hand, shrugged then fetched a beer each for them.

"Thanks!"

"Can we have six?"

He gave them some more.

They both sprinted away with impressive gusto.

Johann shut his door quietly. He would hear them from time to time. He would get up to write on his story that he knew was not that important. He would look up larping on the Enternet. And he would figure out when his next class was, what a syllabus was too. He would take care of his parents and sleep more in his office than his campus apartment. And the larpers would visit him every night and talk about life and he would give them beers from his endless supply. Teaching writing would not be as easy as he thought. There were problem students who came late, didn't read, didn't talk, didn't seem to care, didn't even buy the books. He was drunk most of the time. It was supposed to be a good life, a life to grab, but in the end it just felt small. He felt smaller all the time, never bigger, and it saddened him.

One night the twin larpers knocked on his door and came in and they drank beer. The next thing he knew, he was larping right along with them, running throughout the building, hiding like a little boy in a bathroom stall, getting wacked with objects, out of breath, but feeling deeply good, not absent and not small like he had been feeling.

When he was done larping on another night, weeks later, they walked back with him to the office, all grinning and sweaty. They drank some more Tecate, the red cans reminding him of Christmas for some reason. He had ordered his Lester doll and he put on a ventriloquist's show for them and they loved it. Through Lester's mouth, he told them how he hated faculty meetings and students and classes and that he missed home even though he had hated it when he was there and that the two of them were his friends now and that he liked larping. Nobody else had talked to him since his arrival except for the twins. No other professors had even visited his office to welcome him to the college.

He kept using Lester's mouth to express himself, floating into Spanish at times and at some point he realized that he was crying and laying the doll on his desk, just crying about life itself and what a waste it felt like sometimes, but then there would be moments like this where you were just running with strangers and happy and not thinking about anything at all, and it made you feel better.

Soon, he said goodbye to them. He should write about the twins one day, he thought, staring at lifeless Lester on his desk, shutting the heavy door that kept the room quiet. It could be a happy story, a happy story about Wisconsin.

TOM AND I

I am a lot like Tom. For example, I write. I am writing now. Tom wrote. I have a voice problem. Tom did too, a lisp, and he was not a good speaker. I like black girls. So did Tom. However, I do not like slaves. Let me rephrase. Not that I don't like slaves, per se. But that Tom owned them and didn't give them up when everyone else did. Of course, about twenty percent of the country owned slaves at that time, and that was only out of five million people. Meaning that one million people owned slaves.

I am also bankrupt this year. Tom was a huge debtor, up until the time he died. In fact, during my bankruptcy I learned that it is our right to file for it, and it's in the Constitution. Tom financed the whole Louisiana Purchase on debt.

He liked wine. Although he drank several glasses every night, I heard somewhere that the wine glasses were smaller back then. I like wine when I'm not in AA.

He liked to read and invented a revolving bookshelf in order to keep open and read many books at once, sort of a cabinetry book-tree thing. I read multiple books simultaneously. Of course, I never finish any of them, but the similarity here is *wild*.

He would ice his feet every morning. I ice my feet at night!

He started a free-for-all university in Virginia where students could study whatever they wanted and were under their honor to rat on cheaters. And I applied to U.Va. but was not accepted.

Almost all of his kids practically died.

A son born and dead in 1777.

A daughter, Mary, at twenty-six, dead in 1804.

Jane born in 1774, died in 1775.

Lucy Elizabeth born 1780, died 1781.

Then another daughter born 1782, also named Lucy Elizabeth but who died in 1785.

I never had kids. We differ here. But I know what it's like to lose a lot of people. He was determined though, and naming the two Lucy Elizabeths just breaks my heart sometimes.

On an up note, he wrote the Declaration of Independence. I wrote my own personal Declaration of Independents. Note the "s" difference. I am very independent. So Tom and I are not exactly alike; there are small differences.

He loved his garden. I practically *am* a garden. I have a big one in my back yard.

He died on July 4th. I am not dead yet but that's the day I plan to die.

He was President a couple of times. I was President of the Local Garden Club.

My name is also Tom and I live in Virginia. I sort of look like him.

Basically, I think that I am kin to Tom. Who else could get away with, "All men are created equal [Shouldn't it be *equally*?]" and yet maintain slaves whom he probably slept with and fathered children? Or maybe his brother Randolph sired them. No one knows but the DNA guys, and even they don't seem to know.

Either way, sleeping with black women ran in his family.

I have a black girlfriend. I believe that I inherited this predilection from Tom.

I won the Tom-Look-Alike Contest once, but I had a wig. Tom looks, well, like himself. I tried to find a relative connection with Tom on my dad's side but no luck so far.

Right now I need to ice my feet. The funny thing is that I have always iced my feet, even before I read about the fact that Tom iced his.

■ ■ ■

My girlfriend wishes I would stop saying, "My black girlfriend." She says, "I don't say, 'My Chinese boyfriend.'"

Yes, I am Chinese, yet I have blond hair and green eyes, like Tom. My parents own a Mexican restaurant in our small Virginia town. We are near Poplar Forest where Tom has his vacation home. I was once stung on the bottom of my foot in his yard during a field trip. By a vibrating bee.

Tom speaks to me a lot. He says, *This is your country. It's okay if you have a vocal problem. Black girls are hot and cool at the same time.*

Thanks Tom!

I talk to him at night when I am alone. After I pretend to read my ten books on my revolving book tree while icing my feet, I lie back on my bed and think of his inventions.

The macaroni extruder. Some even say he invented mac and cheese.

The dumbwaiter.

The double-pen copying apparatus.

The new and improved swivel chair.

Spherical sundial.

Pedometer!

I even went up to Monticello once. Ah, Monticello. He was like a mad scientist, answering his door in his robe and slippers. But I wonder why he never gave up his slaves when he saw his next-door neighbors doing it. I went to Monticello with my black gir—Cara. I have a theory. Since he was so poor like most Americans in debt, he couldn't survive without them. He kept most of his slaves through mortgage agreements. But "All men are created equal[ly]"? Come on, Tom! You're equal but you're my slave. What the?

Tom had trouble speaking. I have a hole in my throat, so I sound like a cartoon mouse sucking helium from a balloon, only it's not like that for a few seconds but all the time. They say it is stress from all the deaths I have experienced, like Tom. And also the acid in espresso that I drink endlessly.

Tom, with his lisp, only gave two speeches during his whole presidency. He made them stop doing the State of the Union address in person and it wasn't done again until Woodrow.

Oh Tom. July 4th. You even died right.

Cara and I want kids. We make fun of racist names since she's black and I'm Chinese. You would be surprised how people in southern Virginia have issues with us being together. We get called names on a regular basis. Words like that are dead to us, but we hear them so often that we have to make jokes. Most people don't realize how racist the South still is. Then again, it was okay for the two-term, slave-owning president to write the Declaration of Independence and for Senator Robert Byrd to have been in the KKK.

Anyway, I am half-Chinese with a really white, Navy father. He is a bit of a prick. In fact I hate him. Typical military freak who never figured out that war is the last resort of idiots and small men. I avoid him and sometimes meditate in front of my upside-down mirror, one similar to the one in Monticello.

Tom was very private, like me. When his wife died, he burned all their letters.

As I said, I am bankrupt. I finally moved out of the house at age thirty, although it's really hard to survive these days. Luckily, Tom was a debtor too and that gives me some hope. He said, "Banking establishments are more dangerous than standing armies." I agree with what Tom says here. Score another for Tom!

Now, one thing that does bug me about Tom is that he also said that mixing races "produces a degradation . . ."

I don't like this part of Tom because Cara and I will certainly have a kid that is part-Chinese, part-black. He will be more American than America, an embodiment of all the confusion, invention, debt and many races that somehow seem to get along even after slavery, while the rest of the world is still hacking millions of people to death with machetes.

My parents are mixed races. Maybe Tom knew it all along, that we keep diluting races enough then we will all cycle back to some strange equality. I don't know. I lost three of my brothers, all soldiers, in various wars, wars my father made them fight. I really am more similar to Tom that you might realize.

I think I know about Tom.

He just wanted to hang out in his robe and slippers and ice his feet and read and invent and drink wine and tour around his garden.

He was a hopeful man, hopeful that he would be able to pay his debts and then release his slaves.

Like me, he never made much money.

Personally, I think he just liked his slaves and wanted to be close to them since all his kids were dying so young.

THE EDIBLE HARMONICA

The storyteller is the figure in which
the righteous man encounters himself.

Walter Benjamin,
Illuminations

For six years Eli Lovelace reviewed "fiction for mature women" at *The Scope*, but it wasn't until the drunken novelist from Kentucky smirked at his receding hairline during an interview at Le Cirque (now closed) that he decided a career change was imminent. Eli had written an un-sellable book before becoming a reviewer and, lately, he wondered how he journeyed so far afield of what he thought he was.

Six years of critiquing mediocrity.

However, aliased as a Czech writer named Levant Jarzoveck, he had published a short novel at a small press seven years ago. The book gods had remaindered it in a nanosecond. He never spoke of the publication. Something like eight of them sold. He bought four. Perhaps five. Okay, he bought all eight.

Sipping 72-hour black coffee and under yet another deadline for his Wednesday review, he decided to create a new section that would appear once a month under the title "Revived", in which obscure published writers who were never reviewed would receive one. His first project was to consider his own book, *The Edible Harmonica*, nearly seven years after it entered the stores *sans* review.

Lately, he would hide in one of the newspaper's restroom stalls full of anxiety, hands on thighs bracing his upper body as if he stood in a teamless huddle with himself. The room was silent except for an errant tap coursing over a sink. After emerging, he stared at his image in the mirror above the basin: balding pate and reddened eyes. His beard obfuscated the bottom of his face like fog hides a deer in the road. He suffered from insomnia, sometimes not sleeping for a week then suddenly crashing for two or three days straight. And his clothes smelled. Although he wanted to change them, he lacked the energy and couldn't bear to look at his pale, flaccid flesh. For about a month, he had forgotten how old he was. Then he suddenly remembered: forty-one. This caused him further chagrin.

Doing a job that was not in your heart seemed tantamount to slavery. You could not describe the torpor to your friends because they would only riposte with a lack of sympathy: "Oh, like reviewing is really *that* hard, Eli." Still, something that was not you felt like unctuous maggots squirming and diving upon one another as they gnawed away. How difficult could it be to succeed at the aimed goal, not the accidental one? He had begun to feel as life were pulling him toward the thing he didn't want to be, which is why he came up with "Revived" after the Overstreet interview.

During that meeting with Becky Overstreet at Le Cirque, he stared at her shiny square shopping bags wondering how such an utter imbecile could even write her name much less **two** bestsellers (*Strength of Woman Bear* and *The Man, He Is Your Friend*). And writers were not supposed to shop at Saks!

She chewed with her mouth opening wide, each mastication like galoshes in a puddle. When she ordered lemon sorbet at the end of the meal, she called it "sherbert", as in "Sure, Bert." Feeling contrary, he asked her if the plot of her next novel "was also part of the Oprah-Winfrey oligarchy".

"The wut?"

"Well, who influenced you as a writer?"

"The all-mighty dollar, that's who. Got two drunk ex-husbands and four kids and a Buick payment. Didn't have no privileged life like yourself."

She lifted her sorbet bowl and lapped the surface.

"No love of the craft?"

"Kraft American Cheese maybe. Love the individual slices."

"Jesus," he muttered.

"You payin' for this?"

"Sure. *The Scope* will cover it."

"Tell you what, take my advice and lighten up. You seem bitter as vinegar."

"Excuse me?"

"Maybe you need a wife."

"For *what*?" he said, looking at his watch.

"Little perspective on somebody besides yourself."

"I don't believe this."

"You're just too in love with—"

"You want me to take suggestions from *you*?"

"Smart man takes advice from anybody."

"You aren't even a real writer!" Eli nearly screamed.

He signed for the check as she stood and grabbed her bags. Then she ran her fingers through his thinning hair and said, "I ain't a bald reviewer, at least."

When his review of *The Edible Harmonica* appeared, not only did Eli receive praise for the discovery, but his Levant Jarzoveck royalty checks increased in size and number. A second printing was even issued.

One evening, he opened the mailbox to find a bonus from the newspaper and *two* checks from his publisher—three in *one day*. In celebration he bought some purple vegetables from New Guinea to cook in a stew.

Fellow reviewers at *The Scope* brooded in precise proportion to Eli's sudden surge of success, which increased manifold. The managing editor even put him on salary after nearly a decade of being paid by the word. Lately, he even sensed that one of his jealous colleagues rummaged through his top drawer for change. The tiny Eskimo woman with large hips from Mount Holyoke could not afford the tip when she ordered take-out and he guessed that it might be she. In addition, he knew for a fact that she was unable to discern between *there, their* and *they're*. One morning he tried to explain the difference but she just gazed at him as if he were a zoo animal. Hours later, he tried to figure out what her staring meant. Her disembodied eyes followed him around now and he liked that she had looked at him. He could not remember the last person that had actually stared at him in more than a curious way. Did he imagine that she was saying something with her stare?

Two things struck him suddenly: he had never loved anyone and he did not even know her name. How was it possible to think of her so much? A third thing followed closely: no one had loved him either.

A reviewer was an archeologist. On the other hand, writing that novel was like being the first person to graffito a cave with hieroglyphics. He wanted to be the studied, not the studier. No matter how many credits his job of reviewing received, its debits far outweighed them and he couldn't help but think he was in some horrible debt that had consumed him. *Years* had passed criticizing prosaic texts written by average people and he was beginning to think that he needed to become ordinary as well. Or already had.

If your soul is an iceberg, each thing you did that was contrary to what you were was like a chisel chipping the ice, paring it to nothingness. Although the soul was cold, frozen even, it was at least very big and impressive and looked like it would be there forever.

Right now the iceberg had been reduced to floes. Soon it would evanesce to water.

He remembered hiding in an apartment in the East Village after having written collegiate pabulum for years. Too many parties kept him from the true task. Too many people requesting too much of his time. Determined, he saved his money from the waiter's job he held (and lucked out in an aunt's will) and he hid and bought time. He even created a new identity, having always been fond of disappearing acts.

Perhaps the Czech-ness of metamorphosing from Eli Lovelace to Levant Jarzoveck was the result of reading too many Kundera novels too fast. But people liked his book now. They were reading *The Edible Harmonica*. What a tsunamic irony, he said shaking his head. I caused my own success but now I can't admit it is I.

Then again it might be perfect, he thought. He could keep his solitude and not be fettered by the shallow creek of fame. With writing there was no noise, except for the clicking of keys or the scratching of a pencil, but no music. Goethe, he remembered, said that architecture was frozen music. And writing words was like writing notes. But who ever played words written from a novel? No one. Not anymore at least. There were those awful literati readings, but what were they except cures for insomnia?

He (as Levant) and his agent and publisher negotiated a second book. *The Scope* also wanted to know how Eli discovered Levant and could he get an interview? That was fun—interviewing himself:

Eli: How did you decide to write *The Edible Harmonica*?

Levant: Well, I liked the metaphor of a man who could play a musical instrument that he could also later digest. It spoke to a lot of the political stuff happening in, um, Prague—

Eli: Now, in beginning of the novel, he plays for a long time *then* eats his harmonica. Later, he can only play for a short time before he chows down. By the end, he walks on stage with the band and the last line is, "No music came to him in that moment, only the desire to devour the music before it could be played." I remember reading that part and thinking what a perfect novel this was. I mean, perfect. I'm trying to be objective here, but I think you are the best goddamn writer we have. You never make the harmonica some substance that is palatable. He actually *eats* the metal, breaks teeth and ends up ripping his intestines in the process.

Levant: Yes, what you forgot to mention about that final scene is that he has obviously not been able to excrete any of the harmonicas. They have accumulated in his stomach and so he bleeds in all of his sphincters. And everyone knows that we have three or maybe more sphincters. He has even swallowed his teeth that cracked when chewing the wood and metal. All this stuff exists inside him. The un-digestible.

Eli: You performed quite a disappearing act for many years. Now everyone anticipates your next work. Anything on the horizon?

Levant: Horizon. I hate that word. I started a short story called "The Gelatinous Tank" about a think tank where all the people can contemplate nothing but Jell-O, but I felt like I was just plagiarizing myself. Next, I contemplated the idea of a milk piñata, but that faded as well. So I decided to write about salvation.

Eli: Why?

Levant: Well, it's interesting. I had a discussion with a friend of mine recently. He's one of those writers who doesn't write. You know, always talking about *needing* to *want* to be *able* to write but never doing anything but talking. Anyway, he said my oeuvre (which is only one book) was too full of pain. But I said that it wasn't. Like that final scene, for example. He knows he's bleeding inside. He knows his life is absurd. Gradually losing the ability to play music combined with a madness to eat harmonicas until death— this is not pain. It's a big picture of life.

Eli: Of course, of course.

Levant: But there is no love. He's right about that.

Eli: So . . .?

Levant: Why not, I said to myself, write about the same character being rescued. Being operated on. Fixing his insides. And meeting someone devoted enough to see him through it. She would have to be a cook. A cook would feed him the right things. She would change his whole appetite and save him. Anyway, that's my next book.

As he wrote the interview, Eli came up with the idea for the second novel. After turning in the dialogue to his editor, he called his publisher who was about to send him a contract. His agent had reviewed it and given him the yes. Thank god he had never met these people in person, a privacy he had guarded well (aided by his agoraphobia possessed since childhood).

His editor loved the interview. For the next five months he put aside "The Gelatinous Tank" and wrote *The Cook Saves the Music*. When it came out the following year, he, of course, reviewed it for the front page of the Sunday *Scope*:

By now we all know of the resurgence of Levant Jarzoveck. When I reviewed *The Edible Harmonica* two years ago, it was only after I had discovered it on a remainder table at The Strand. It was almost as if I had written the book myself, as if it were my own voice reading my own words. It is a mistake to talk about an author's past in terms of his new work, but that is impossible when it comes to reviewing *The Cook Saves the Music*, Jarzoveck's sequel to *The Edible Harmonica*.

The story begins at the end of the last book, that memorable scene in which Seth Grace, who plays before he eats his instrument, has reached a gruesome point:

"He held the harmonica to his lips but they did not touch it. He opened his mouth. The audience heard his teeth bite metal. Everyone winced when he swallowed it and grabbed his stomach and fell to the floor. Half the audience came to hear him play and hoped he would stop hurting himself. The other half came to watch him do this very thing, this circus act that he could not control. He held his stomach. He was torn. He could feel the tears. No music came to him in that moment, only the desire to devour the music before it could be played."

Now, in this follow-up novel, the cook, a young Eskimo woman, rushes to the stage in the first sentence and touches him. As he fades from consciousness, he feels her:

"The metal in his stomach filled him. She held his hand and instead of the crowd caring, it dissipated like a group that knows its team has lost and it would rather be the first out of the parking lot than be supportive. Then it was the two of them. Even the band left, so accustomed to Seth Grace."

What is striking about this novel is growth from absurdity into love. Every young writer seems to fear connection and yet here is someone who will not accept tragedy for his character, his surrogate. Giving Seth Grace a new life and a new book and feeding him, as he needs to be fed, satisfies the reader like a perfect meat with perfect wine. Without spoiling a certain scene, I will say that it, once again, involves a final meal of harmonicas that is either eaten or not. Read to see. This is the most flawless book I have ever read. I read it six times and have purchased several copies for my close relatives.

By then everybody wanted to know Levant's whereabouts. Since Eli was the only one who knew them, he had sole interview privileges, which he free-lanced for various magazines. Then came the nomination for the National Book Award. He was a finalist but didn't win. Eli breathed a sigh of relief. A further annoyance ensued when Vaclav Havel got his phone number and wouldn't stop calling.

His publisher wanted a photo for *The Cook Saves the Music*, but Eli assured him that Levant's face was not a good selling point. Sometimes he forgot who he was and strolled in the Sheep's Meadow to clear his head. Or listened to music somewhere. One afternoon he caught the movie *Shh! The Octopus* at the Angelika then saw a band called Bottlecap at Reggie's on W. 41st near Penn Station. Three guys from Virginia.

During his walk home to the Lower East Side, he decided that he was a fraud and maybe even bored, plus he wanted to *tell someone* about his ruse. The game was no longer more fun than the writing itself. Sooner or later he would be caught in the lie, so he needed to end it quickly. Subtract the fun and he realized he was not much more than a cheat.

Unfortunately, a contract for a third book surfaced. Would they find his apartment building, he wondered? Paranoia ate at him (those maggots again). His agent, publisher, personal editor and *Scope* boss began to suspect him more when Eli reviewed Jarzoveck's third: *Memoirs of Kundera's Second Cousin Twice-Removed on His Mother's Side: The Sagacious Lip Reader.*

In a moment of irritation he penned the following:

> Well, well, well, the mysterious Czech stylist appears again, this time with a non-fiction family history masquerading as a latent French misanthropic pseudo-realist black comedy that makes Moliere look like Voltaire.
>
> "What?" you say.
>
> Exactly. Or as the French say, "Exactement."
>
> This purposeful anti-narrativistic intractability equates to a smug contempt toward the reader. Whereas in his last two texts *The Edible Harmonica* and *The Cook Saves the Music*, one sees allegory, symbol and mythology baked into one cookie; one now has a whole plate of cookies—and not chocolate chip!
>
> Here is the recrudescent plot: A small French boy from the Cote D'Azur thinks he is related to Kundera. He goes on a journey to Paris or wherever the hell Milan (Kundera, not Italy) is. During this journey he discovers the European theater (blatant litotes referring to the war in Belgrade!) and lands a job as the director of Ionesco's *Rhinoceros* whilst vacationing in Nice.
>
> Because he has no idea what he is doing, he keeps calling his mother who eventually tells him that the whole Kundera relation was fabricated to get free copies of *The Book of Laughter and Forgetting*.
>
> Distraught, the boy builds a "literary time machine" wherein he morphs into the persona of Albert Camus, experiences the plot of *The Stranger* and right after he

shoots the guy on the beach runs back to his device and becomes the Little Prince.

As you can see Jarzoveck toys with us with his non-committal, overly-creative scenarios, distancing himself emotionally like two doomed ships that pass in the night. Pretty soon this guy needs to stop writing because, frankly, I think he's become as cocksure as a college athlete.

And, in truth, he *has* stopped writing.

Naturally, I write these words with regret because Levant Jarzoveck, in fact, just died last Thursday and thus will not be able to write any more books. He was knocked from his French bicycle by an unfresh—and hence very hard—baguette that had been nailed unsuspectingly to a telephone pole. Although he didn't perish immediately, no one found him for six days because his green clothing resembled the grass too much and many folks thought he was a large shrub.

The death occurred in Montreal where he had been residing for many years, contrary to what many thought. I received this information in the strictest confidence and regret conveying such horrible news, especially within the aegis of a literary review, but I'm sure it's what Levant would have wanted, being one of the few privileged people who knew and loved him.

A few weeks later an agent approached Eli about a biography. He also received countless screenplays about Levant (*Czech Please, Czech Mix, That Deserves a Czech*) but ignored them until they stopped coming. Then some freak calling himself Levant Jarzoveck began to frequent the office pretending to be the actual author. At first he thought it was Vaclav Havel harassing him again. In any case it was really too much and became even worse when the publishers were so suspicious that they ended up discovering his trick:

"*Scope* Reviewer Lovelace Fired, Faces Fraud Charges"

When the story appeared in the paper, it led to severe depression and fear that he would be sued. But the books began to sell like crazy and he still received money for them. They were, after all, decent. The process still unraveled him and he couldn't leave the apartment. Even though he stopped reviewing, he still huddled with himself. He forgot the sound of his own voice. He kept thinking of the Eskimo editor and seeing her disembodied eyes. That staring. His stomach was empty too, filled with a hunger that could not be helped.

In his spare time he tended his small garden on the balcony and whenever the occasional reporter skulked into his building and attempted to question him about the controversy, he would aim a shotgun at him and through a megaphone shout, "You are trespassing. I am the Little Prince. I am the Stranger. I am Candide!"—a refrain that he muttered incessantly.

One Year Later

In the Levant autobiography that Eli wrote but once again fabricated, the first lines read, "Writing is malady from which I create plans to escape daily." Some days he wasn't sure *who* he was. He believed more people were following him and he needed to finish this autobiography before they came! The door buzzer gyrated his nerves. He heard footsteps—how did they get past the guard? He had just about reached a true panic when he caught someone running from his door, having slipped a note under the crack. In his robe he chased a person who looked to be a she. It was a Saturday morning in the Village and everyone seemed asleep. A small Mexican boy on a stool at a deli cut honeydew and placed the pieces in plastic cups. He stole one of the pieces of fruit as he ran to catch the woman who had slid the note under his door. As he chewed the honeydew, he loved how cold it was sliding down his throat.

Eli noticed her hustle into a music store and he followed quickly. Nowhere to go, she pretended to view a used Hall and Oates LP. It was the Eskimo critic. He stared at her. What did she want with her squirrel face and twitching nose? Maybe a year had passed since their last meeting, one time when he had walked near the office. At that moment, they had exchanged no greetings and passed each other like strangers. But when he turned to see if it was really she who had passed him, she had stopped and looked at him. He stopped too. But then he had become so afraid that he turned quickly and walked away fast.

One thing bothered him, though, and he wanted to very much ask her: Had they still had not fixed the leaky spigot at the office? She glanced at him, lifting her head in his direction. There was no recognition, not even scorn. It dawned on him that he had never cleaned out his desk and he suddenly saw it before him: the paper clips, the coins, the erasers, the stacks of books to be reviewed, the stained Styrofoam cups, his name carved with a razor blade in the wood: Eli Lovelace.

Approaching her he said there was probably five dollars in change in his top drawer. It was hers. She could have it. Have a nice meal on him. She smelled very clean. Why was she sneaking around his apartment? What did her note say?

Hello. It just said hello, Eli, and maybe we could have coffee sometime and catch up. That's all.

Well, why run then? he wondered.

Feeling an ache in his chest and touching her shoulder, he told her she could have whatever she needed.

"Eli . . ." she said.

He expected her to flee but she remained and they held this tableau for a few moments: a man in a robe far from himself with many months of gin wafting from his mouth, a slight woman with disproportionate hips and a twitching nose hoping to sober him a bit, saying his name once then again more softly, a quiet engine reminding him of his name.

They stood amid all the music with none playing because, on this particular Sunday, the nose-ringed store manager wanted to finish a novel he was reading and didn't want the noise to distract him. Oddly enough, he was reading *Edible Harmonica*. Summoning perhaps the last bit of nerve in his stomach, Eli took in a breath and asked her if she would like to maybe go eat somewhere together. She nodded. And as they walked together to find a place for brunch, Eli thought that he would worry about one thing at a time, ask for her name a little later.

SHOW DOG

A freshly shaven scrotum stared at Rand Scofield like two Peter Lorre eyes.

"God," he mumbled to himself. "They're just hanging there."

The poodle stood obediently on the table. The groomsgirl shaped its legs, chest and upper waist into white cotton candy fluff but left the hind legs and genitals bare. The tail had poofs then was bald. Several yellow bows were tied around a head that looked like a magician's twist balloon.

Rand had wandered into the dog show by accident, relieved that he missed his technical expo that was just upstairs. The convention center was so large and he had been lost all week, if you wanted to know the truth.

Tired of not knowing where he was, he found a wall map. He had even been getting off on the wrong floors in the Chicago Hotel where he was staying. He would be on the elevator one moment—then in front of someone's door (that was not his) the next. Once, he had even gotten off five floors too early. The same thing kept happening at the convention. What was a businessman but a useless accumulation of meetings, phone calls and letters anyway?

He was *supposed* to interact with the computer resellers, vendors, systems integrators, as well as attend sessions with CEOs, in addition to working a booth of his own company. He watched demonstrations of software. He exchanged cards with people he would never call or email. He spoke the inane business phrases like *Return on Investment, Increased Sales Revenue* and *Market Share* that held no meaning. He checked his messages back home over twenty times a day just to have the pleasure of deleting them. He wished he could delete the actual person leaving the message by pressing #7. He wished that he could delete all the events in his life until now, except his wife Anne. He wanted to delete Rufus because his son stole all the private moments with her. He wanted to delete his career, which he *had* to begin because of Rufus the Accident. Rand was the walking business dead.

Mostly he watched all the eyes of the crowd become the same listless face. It stared at him. In a language that was absent of something necessary, the mouth on the face whispered to him that he did not belong, nor could he escape. He found himself at the grooming area almost as if he had been picked up like a chess piece and moved.

Ten feet away was a competition for Schnauzers. A booth with bronze statues of dogs caught his eye in the distance. All of the women with golden retrievers seemed to have blond hair. A smiling border collie trotted past him. A robust older woman led two sniffing bloodhounds, one a puppy, one full-grown. A St. Bernard butted the head of one of its kin and woofed then pounced on nothing.

"What kind of poodle is it?" Rand asked the groomer.

"Standard," she said, snipping ear hairs. The white dog could have been a vivisected sheep, raw pink in areas and fluffy like a cloud in others.

"Thanks," he said, thinking what the hell is a *standard* poodle?

He walked to the dog food section and tasted a piece, much to the surprise of the man in charge of the table. Billboard-size checkered banners hung from the ceiling announcing PURINA. This building, just one part of the convention center, reminded him of an airplane hangar. And the area upstairs with the software tables was even grander, maybe twice the size of the dog-show hall.

Three whippets, lithe with suspended tails, pulled a woman behind them. There was so much movement. Each type of dog had its own competition area and he didn't want to leave.

A week had gone by and he hadn't truly spoken to anyone. Except for the canned demos and gladhanding, he felt as if he had said nothing. The words came out of him like a yawn. But he was forty-seven and he was so used to the invisible speaking that it gave him comfort in the end. Nothing was visible anymore.

If his gray office in Kansas City ever became too dull, which was every third day, he simply took a trip like this one and revived his energies. But something, what *was* it, kept him from feeling refreshed this time.

Maybe these dogs.

Those poodle balls were striking and really disturbing. They hung there, vulnerable and skinned. The poor dog had to just take it while the grooming person did the job. The poor poodle had a look of resignation, pride and stupidity, and his eyes almost appeared aware that something wasn't right.

Rand squatted to pet an Akita whose owner explained the excessive shedding. "They have two coats and—well, see, look at your suit."

Rand brushed away the wisps of hair and smiled. "Who's a good dog?" he said, petting the top of the head. "Who's a *good* dog?"

He made his way through all the competitions. Owners on leashes walked in squares as judges scored them for heeling properly. An Australian shepherd's tongue hung to the side and Rand admired the calico array of colors. He asked if it were a border collie but the man said no, pointing out the lack of tail.

He sensed himself much more, the more he moved and touched things. He knew that he liked this room better than the one upstairs. He liked these dogs and people moving around so proudly, so clean, so smart and so alive, and he wondered how many thick tufts and ticks and mites and fleas surrounded his heart. Much more, he wondered how you groomed it; he didn't know how. He recognized that while he didn't hurt, he didn't feel good either. I'm just not anything, he admitted silently to himself.

He thought of his wife and wanted to go home and take a drive with her, but lately she had been on the phone all the time with her half-brother, Marland, and he thought something was amiss. She didn't seem to want to take drives anymore.

Pretty soon he needed to go upstairs.

He had to be in his booth in fifteen minutes. In that time he touched as many dogs as he could. He talked to owners and admired their purpose.

After a while he returned to the same poodle and noticed something that he hadn't seen previously. There were ten tables, all with poodles on them, each shaven in different ways and colors: black, white and pantyhose brown.

"Why do they take such a beautiful animal and make it look so ugly?" he thought.

As he passed them, they stared back at him with what he thought were sad eyes. He stopped to pet a curly black one that licked his hand like an old woman in a rest home reaching out her arm to a stranger.

Returning to the hotel in the cab later that night, he reflected on the dog show. In the elevator, when the doors closed, he sang, "Some day, when you're awfully low . . ." but stopped the very second the doors opened.

As he wandered around the halls he came to his room (definitely his) and he inserted the card key. Inside, he sat at his desk and was sure of one thing: he was going back to the dog show in the morning. He was going back this time because he wanted to—not because he was lost.

■　■　■

In the morning, he turned on the television and watched the Latino version of *Charlie's Angels*. He checked his email, used the television to calculate his room bill. He decided to go ahead and do his expense report. He taped receipts onto the page, filled in all the blanks in Excel and ordered some room service—French toast, coffee, grapefruit. While he waited for his food, he showered and shaved, dressed and packed, stealing two bars of milled soap. He would carry his bag with him to the expo and check it with his overcoat then go to the airport after the press conference with that jejune entrepreneur. Entremanure. Investment wanker.

His food arrived and he asked the porter to place the tray on the bed. He peeled the plastic from the grapefruit. The French toast was moist. He poured a cup of coffee that was silky black and steaming hot.

Let's see, he needed to remain at his software booth for two hours. One of the marketing girls would pack up the machines and advertising posters. He glanced at his watch and stared at the ceiling trying to calculate how much time he needed to go from the expo to O'Hare. After a couple of bites of the toast he found it palatable. He ignored eating the grapefruit but pressed his finger right into it then licked the tip.

Outside the hotel he stepped into a cab on Michigan Avenue that took him to the front of the Convention Center. Inside the building he checked his bag and wool overcoat with the two women who carried on an argument about jellybeans while they dealt with him, even dropping his clothing at one point.

Now, he said aloud, where's that wall map? Ah. He walked to a stone kiosk and checked his location. To insure that he made it to the right area, he even asked a docent with a walkie-talkie who mumbled too many directions too quickly. Once again, he returned to the map when she wasn't looking. YOU ARE HERE. No kidding. But where do I go from here?

He ascended the escalator, walking once or twice. At the top there were more stairs, more escalators, a food court and the din of noise coming from somewhere. After he had glanced at his watch again, he walked right back to the dog show. He wanted to find the poodles.

A huge Great Dane with no leash trotted past him.

Where were all the dogs?

In fact, where were their owners?

Why was that big dog alone?

Perhaps he needed to find one of the security guards. He watched the lone animal sniff the air and open its mouth and chomp on what he guessed it thought was a fly. Rand Scofield needed to demonstrate his software in a few minutes, but there were no shaved dogs, no judges, no owners.

Upstairs, the acned marketing girls shouted into microphones about three-tiered, backup-and-recovery software storage models, not knowing what they meant but still trying to convey authenticity and excitement. The overweight salesmen smiled and prayed the other salespeople were not smarter than they were. The CEOs posed proudly, heads high. The security guards sniffed for people without badges. The young analysts laughed with each other.

Who was judging them?

Down here they touched the dogs. They made them beautiful. They trained them. There was delight even when the big room was empty. He could feel the pride. When the software expo ended there would be nothing, just an empty room that people could not wait to leave.

After the show, the cab, the flight and the limo to his house in Kansas City, he dropped his bag in the living room, grabbed a pair of scissors and headed to the bathroom.

He closed the door, stripped and sat in the tub.

For the next two hours he snipped the hairs as well as the parsley tufts of pubes. Then he found his razor and shaved the whole area. He thought he heard his annoying son Rufus, but it was just his imagination. If there ever was a kid who was nothing like him, it had to be Rufus. The boy sounded like he had chewed up about seven dictionaries. One morning, he could have sworn he looked just like Marland, his wife's half-brother. He considered the thought for a moment. Sadly, if it were true, he didn't care anymore.

His work was nothing important and the illusion that he was such a fantastic businessman was mostly air. Worst of all, he felt beyond the ability to change anything about anything. And anyway, he would be on another plane soon.

Once he was done, he stood and looked down at himself. The hair cascaded onto the tub as he stepped onto the floor. In his bedroom, he flashed his rear at the full-length mirror on his closet door and examined his testicles thinking that if he were a poodle, he could definitely compete. He could prance like the best of them. Hell, he would win.

As he exited the bathroom, he ran into his son who had been standing at the door.

"Rufus, I thought I heard you."

"Hi Father."

"Stop calling me Father," he requested.

"Where you going next?"

"California," Rand told him.

"What's in California?" his son asked.

"Business."

Rufus stared at him and remained in the doorway with his arms folded, implying *why are you never here.*

"I'm home now, aren't I?"

"I guess."

"Excuse me, son, I need to go to bed."

"Yessir."

The next morning in his seat on the plane, feeling dehydrated but continuing to drink the coffee that parched him, he thought of his boy. He didn't know what to say to him or what his life was like. How old was he? He couldn't even remember. I think he's finishing the tenth grade.

A nasal-voiced steward announced how to put on a seat belt as a stewardess gave the demonstration. This was a performance Rand had seen enough. He checked his seat belt, though, and it was secure. Then he pulled out an in-flight magazine and began the crossword puzzle, which someone else had started. As his pen printed the letters in the squares, the plane backed up and taxied to the runway. He looked out the window to the tarmac and saw a man motioning with orange reflectors in his hands. He noticed a fuel truck drive past the plane. Then the captain spoke and said they were four deep.

Rand lifted his arm, tilted his wrist, looked at his Rolex. It was 8:16 a.m. He sat in business class and reclined his leather seat. An attendant that he knew brought him a complimentary gin and tonic and he sipped at the plastic cup. He was in the middle area of the section.

As the plane rose, his drink began to spill on his white shirt cuff. The wheels came up and he felt them underneath the aircraft. That was always his cue to unbuckle his seat belt, which he did. But everything started to go backward. The attendants were falling toward him. It felt like the plane was tilting almost straight up in the air. People began to drop from their seats, including him. His legs came over his head and landed on the floor behind him. A body sailed over his head and splatted into the lavatory. Newspapers were blowing everywhere like a windy day. Magazines slid under him. He covered his head and the plane continued to plummet.

It seemed as if the plane was exactly vertical and everyone was dropping to the bottom. Some rolled, some were in the air, some held on and then let go. His head was about to explode. For some reason he was able to hold onto his crossword puzzle, but when he saw that he still had it, he tossed it. Being in the middle kept him from falling all the way down one of the aisles like many others. The plane stopped its vertical rise and the whole thing dropped. Breaths of relief came when the gravity changed. Then more gasps.

As it fell, bottom first, the plane's nose tried to right itself. The nose fell into a dive and Rand was knocked forward into his seat. There was nothing to grip. The people that he had seen fall to the aft area were now returning to the fore. Through his shock, he found himself crying and being pulled around the plane as other passengers fell on him. One young lady's high heel caught him in the thigh. He was amazed that he heard no sounds even though there were thousands. At the moment of impact, Rand's teeth crunched together and there were few thoughts going through his mind except the dog show. His head hit hard and his last thoughts were of those marvelous, obedient poodles.

STAGGERING ALTITUDES:
The Tragedy of Allard Harcourt

"Hi folks. We should get to talk to Allard Harcourt in a second. Here he is. Allard. How do you think you played tonight?"

"Well, Mike, my teammates seemed to find the locus of preternatural playing ability, and that prowess, combined with—"

"Um . . . ha ha. You were AWESOME on defense."

"Thanks, thanks, but our team seminars on ontology helped. So did Aristotle's notion of matter and form, you know, hylomorphism, which of course changed with Heidegger's theories abjuring St. Thomas Aquinas for relying on the classics, simply because they were, you know, the classics."

"When you creamed that slam dunk attempt. Whoooooa!"

"To be honest, although the game impels me toward a Zen-like athleticism, it is really the confluence of Platonic mind, body and soul *after the game* where I find myself attaining various levels of Nirvana simultaneously."

"Hey, I don't know what that means!"

"And during the game, I like to call myself an inventor."

"An inventor?" the announcer said, becoming more bemused by the minute.

"Yes, for example, tonight, you couldn't tell, but I invented a new algorithm for the enhancement of Malthusian hunger charts, all when I simply readjusted my genitalia after a big lay-up."

"Well, that's all we have time for. Thanks Allard."

"Oh, one last thing, to all my fans," said Allard, pointing passionately at the camera, "read the new Stanislav Rellman book on philosophical vocabulary in every day life. It is mindblowing." Allard touched his head with both hands as if to simulate a bomb going off in his head; he was *that* into the most recent Rellman. "Mindblowing," he added again.

"Let's maybe go back to the guys in the booth," the announcer said, practically running his hands across his throat to end the horrendous interview.

"Algorithm"? "Malthusian"? "Ontology"? Holy crap, he hated interviewing Allard. First because he understood about every tenth word that he used. Second because Allard was eight feet tall, exactly, so Mike Chapman, who was five feet tall, exactly, had to hold the microphone up to Allard as if he were a little kid reaching up to a horse with a carrot.

Allard Harcourt waved to the camera, touched his heart with his hand with a peace sign, then moved the peace sign up to his mouth and kissed it and then moved the peace sign right up to the camera.

Off-camera, Mike Chapman rolled his eyes. When the camera was back on him (doing a pan down to accommodate for his height), he sighed and said, "Well, guys, once again we couldn't get a sensible word out of Allard tonight."

"Yep," said the old white-haired announcer with the fake teeth whose name Mike could never remember. He had played professional basketball back in the 1400s and held the record for the most injuries in a season: 312. "Sounds like he had a bulimic binge on a dictionary then puked it up words all over himself."

"That's about right," Mike replied.

"Ha ha ha!" the other announcer guffawed. She was the first lesbian announcer in the N.B.A. "He sure can talk. Whew."

They were all buying time because they knew how Allard Harcourt stole the show and reduced the announcers to "stultifyingly tepid dysphasics" (a phrase he had once used to describe them in a sports editorial).

"Quite a game," the white-haired man said.

"Yes," Mike replied, but thought to himself, *Who won?*

■ ■ ■

Meanwhile, Allard Harcourt, making his slow way the locker room, had stopped to sign some beleaguering autographs. *Not again.* Fans were obligatory evils in this game that he loved. At least I get paid for playing, he thought. In the phalanx of young children, a little white boy in the front row reached out a pad and pen for Allard to sign. Allard squatted waaay down and looked the boy right in the eyes and said, "You want me to sign this?"

The boy nodded with vigor.

"Okay, I will, as long you answer a question for me."

The boy, speechless, nodded again.

"Can you name one contemporary black philosopher?"

The boy turned back to his father who shrugged.

"No," said the boy. "I don't know."

"Aw, that's too bad. Well, research that and I'll sign it next time."

"Research?" the father said. "He's nine."

"Try to get him to think about the racial implications of the intelligentsia instead of giving him that Bob the Builder crap."

Allard ignored the rest of the outstretched arms and pads and pens as if they were tentacles of an octopus about to ensnare him. Then he ducked under the low doorframe and headed down the hallway to his locker feeling dejected that the world could be so much smarter if it tried. Instead, it, the world, went to mindless games that he played and endorsed. His dreams of becoming a Socratic philosopher had been undercut by his father and mother, who because of their ongoing poverty and living in one of the worst projects of Detroit, said to him one night, "You will play basketball. God gave you eight feet, not eight brains."

He sat in front of his locker. They had won tonight. Won what? Another game sponsored by rich nabobs who knew nothing of the ravages on his body. But his mind stayed pure even when his knees cracked and buckled and blew, when the balls of his feet felt like nails were hammered into them.

In life, you were a player, a fan or an announcer.

If nothing else, he liked the metaphor of basketball. He was a player and not a fan. That was good. Actually, he hated watching basketball. He was not an announcer either. Announcers were all nice enough, he supposed, but they were walking, brainless idiots except for Bob Costas.

The t.v. men and women talked about their latest plastic surgeries and how they looked on camera. There were a few avid announcers who knew their stats, but so what. Who gave a damn about basketball stats? Add up that knowledge and how did it contribute to humanity!

He slammed shut his locker. "Screw this," he said, and made his decision as he took a long, warm shower. He had to stand on his sore knees since the stupid shower heads were so low.

The next morning he called the general manager and the coach and told him he was quitting and would work out a reasonable contractual settlement where the team was not affected by his leaving.

"You can't quit!" Coach Little screamed at him, adding, "You're too tall to quit."

"I have to. I'm a little soul sick these days."

"Soulsick!? Jesus Christ. Please tell me that has something to do with your shoes. Please!"

"I can't do it anymore. It's killing me after every game. I'm getting depressed. Plus I'm a free agent anyway."

The arguments lasted for weeks and he still had to play while they were discussing the final outcome. He knew they prolonged it just to keep him until the playoffs. In the end, he agreed to play out the season and that would be it.

During the last forty games he was listless on the court, yet his integrity kept him from quitting. He cared about his team (not the game) and knew that they cared about him—albeit only in a superficial way. So he played hard, against his will.

After every game he slept for seventeen hours while becoming more and more depressed. At eight feet he had been 280 pounds. Now he was sliding down to 240. His mind felt lean and he ignored his body. He did not wrap his ankles or knees. On away trips he sat in the back of the plane and read as much as he could. If he was not reading, he was sleeping. But he didn't eat. And yet he played better and better, mostly, he believed, because his mind was sharp. No one talked to him. He refused interviews. He did his job and saved his money.

Of course they ended up making the playoffs. Since he didn't care, he knew they would. It was always the case: when you wanted something and made that known, the world laughed a little, pretended to give it to you then took it away at the last minute. When you didn't want something, though, the world got intrigued and gave it to you simply because you were not asking.

It was during the third playoff game that Allard had his epiphany and couldn't take it anymore. He had seen Plato's sun outside the cave and now it was time to tell all the chained prisoners about it. During the half-time circus act, he limped into the middle of the court with weak kneecaps, grabbed the announcer's microphone and began to speak.

"Ladies and gentleman, thank you for coming tonight, but I do need to make some quick comments while I have your attention. First, please stop eating all of the terrible food and bad beer that they serve at these games. Not only do you create a lot of trash, you are harming your often average-looking bodies. Secondly, please stop coming to basketball games and instead join a church or help some hungry people. Watch basketball on television, sure, yet please stop encouraging this athletic slave narrative. Thank you!"

By this point his coach had come out of the locker room having learned what was happening. He jogged out to the court and escorted Allard back to the bench. They sat together. "Allard, what the f bomb, man!"

"What?"

"You know what."

"You can't just say that stuff."

"Why not, Coach?"

"Um, you sound insane?"

"I feel like I'm going insane." He dug a finger into each ear and vibrated them around to drown out all people for a moment.

"Well, wait until the playoffs are done. We could go all the way."

"I don't want to 'go all the way,'" Allard informed him.

"Don't you want to be a winner?"

"A winner? Of a bunch of basketball games?"

"Yeah!"

"No!"

The coach stared at Allard as if his player had about eleven noses. In this moment, Allard Harcourt realized something: he hated basketball. Abhorred it. He didn't like the other players and he loathed all the running up and down the court when he could have been doing a Ph.D. or simply studying on his own.

One time, when he was resting on the bench, he pulled out a copy of John McWhorter's *Losing the Race: Self-Sabotage in Black America*. The camera zeroed in on him sitting and reading, while his teammates jumped and yahooed for their fellow players. Thereafter, he was deemed a non-team player. When interviewed on ESPN about the matter, he shrugged and said, "Bench-time is the only time I get to read."

"But you're a paid professional athlete."

"Big deal. I can't read on a bench?"

The interviewer was flummoxed for a moment. He was used to the canned post-game responses, dropping quarters into the player: "Yeah, um, you know, well, I just got out there and played the best I could and I did it for God and my mom and, you know, we didn't win but maybe we'll win the next time for Jesus, but I don't care because I just made about $600,000 for about two hours of work. Hollllah!"

After that half-time lecture, Allard was suspended from the playoffs. A couple guys from the team called him at home and left long, excoriating messages about failing "the brotherhood". Allard stopped eating altogether. He was morose about how much time he had squandered doing something that he was good at but by no means liked. And he assumed that he had loved it! How could he not have realized this sooner?

He went online and checked all his accounts to see how much money he actually had. The next day he called his lawyer, his accountant and agent. He wanted to ask them a bunch of questions, questions that had lingered with him on the road in the lonely buses (when he had tried to read and his teammates made fun of him).

He didn't like to sleep with groupies.

He didn't like to curse.

He didn't believe in God like all of them claimed to believe.

He simply liked reading and thinking and asking questions about his life. He wanted the world to question itself too.

On one trip a couple guys leaned over their seats and pestered him.

"Why you read all the time?" one pried.

"Why are you such a colossal moron of banality?" he replied.

"Hey now. Don't be usin' words I don't understand."

"Leave me alone," Allard threatened. "Before I strangle each of you while laughing maniacally."

They left him alone.

■ ■ ■

His suspension would keep him out of the playoffs. He was done! No returning in the fall, no matter how much his coaches and team wanted him. Of course it took him a moment or two to absorb this new freedom.

He slept late.

He pulled books off his shelf that he had never read but always wanted to.

And this is what happened to Allard Harcourt.

He kept forgetting to eat.

Each day he read a new book.

And each day he realized more and more that a life is nothing but time and action. His actions had been superfluous to this point.

As he read more and missed meals, he dropped another thirty pounds. He was now at 210.

"Jesus," he said, looking at the mirror one morning.

He wouldn't leave his house.

He ordered books online.

Six months passed before he spoke to anyone.

It was his coach calling him again and he finally answered.

"Allard! We're all worried about you."

He was almost too weak to answer. "I'm having a hard time," he replied. "But happy."

He hung up the phone slowly and collapsed, smashing his head on the corner of his kitchen table.

Many days went by before he became conscious enough to call 911.

His head was not right; it never had been. But now he could remember nothing. In the hospital the doctors and nurses all recognized him, but he had no idea what they meant. He didn't even know what "basketball" was. They turned on the television for him and he watched his old team play.

"Basketball," he muttered in the bed. "Weird."

"You're in the N.B.A., bro!"

"What is the orange hoop there?" he said, pointing at the t.v.

"The rim?"

"Hm. The rim."

"And below that is the net."

"A strange game."

His coach brought him books from the house and he read. One morning he overheard the doctor say that he had never seen such a case. *Baffling*. But Allard's mind was clearer now and the only thing that filled his brain was book after book, one after another.

After a few weeks in the hospital, he returned home. As he stood by himself in the middle of his modest eleven-million-dollar mansion, he began to cry, at first only from his eyes but then throughout his body. His neck craned backward and he closed his eyes tightly. He gripped his fists and screamed a scream of a man who has found and lost himself at the same time, and also a man who has learned that his life is merely a precious piece of time. Somewhere deep in him, the memory of what he had lost began to surface like a slow whale. He had lost time. He remembered what he had forgotten, some of it, enough to make him deeply saddened by what he had wasted. Basketballs bounced on the hard floors of his head, thumping repeatedly, and the anguish that ensued was something he could grip in his hands. Screams rose from his legs and traveled through him and his mouth. His mouth stayed open, motionless as his body broke down. He leaned on a wall. He was alone, wailing in silence. At this precise moment, his cell phone rang. It was the guy who kept calling himself "Coach".

"Allard?"

He tried to speak.

"Can you talk? Are you home from the hospital?"

He just couldn't.

"You can't keep holing yourself up like this."

Allard hung up the phone feeling a mute despair.

After another week, Allard found the strength to go to a therapist. While he sat there, the therapist, a black male like himself, asked him soft questions about his state of mind, his emotions.

"I feel as if I do not know myself. The only food for me is books. I am remembering more of my fall, or falls really. The first from basketball, the second one more literal. I don't mind being fallen. But I feel lost. Books don't even add up to what I thought they would, even though I love to finish one. People disappoint me too much. I used to be focused on bettering my race and now I'm just a self-absorbed person who bemoans my lost past."

"And," said the therapist, "do you have a plan?"

"I don't," Allard said. "I have no plan at all."

Two Years Later

Mike Chapman had finally located his subject for a magazine interview. Allard Harcourt had disappeared with all his money and had not been discovered until that day. According to rumors, Allard had become a self-described "literary" writer whose sole objective was to "never get published".

Chapman had made it his dogged goal to find the man. He was in Mexico in a small village on the eastern coast and had to travel by local train and bus to find the place. He came to a restaurant on a dirt street and entered through a constellation of flies bouncing around him. There was Allard sitting quietly reading. Mike reached out his hand to greet him. They shook hands.

Allard pulled out his tape recorder.

"It's a story," said Allard. "One sentence. On tape."

"Okaay," said Mike.

"I'll play it for you."

And this is what Mike heard:

"I can't even quit with any sense of finality."

Allard handed Mike the tape recorded story and rose.

"Now, don't stop me," were his last words.

He towered over the table and had to duck as he exited the low doorframe.

Mike tailed him and watched him walk down the dirt street toward the beach.

It was said that Mike also followed him to the beach and on the beach stood watching as Allard walked into the toothpaste blue water and continued to walk until he disappeared, his head sinking.

It was also said that at the last moment Allard surged from the water, did a pretend reverse slam dunk, raised his hands in some sort of personal victory and this time kept walking and sinking for good.

THE X-RATED CHRONICLES OF UNTENURED PROFESSOR, DR. FORD HARRIS

After many years of initially excitable but thereafter indifferent literary agents; and after acquiring the requisite graduate degrees to teach at a university but having no published book; and after succumbing to bankruptcy and, now, imminent foreclosure, Dr. Ford Harris had ceded from the literary world by giving up the notion that he would ever become a respected writer.

For many years he subsisted on illusion (and loans from friends) and occasional editing jobs for middle-aged men and women. He could only seem to publish in the smaller journals that paid in copies. Even his shoulder-sagging agent barely returned his calls or four-page letters these days.

"Fiction is not only dead," said his agent. "It was cremated about twelve years ago."

Dr. Ford Harris's latest teaching job was about to end in June, another non-tenured one. At least this time he had an office and some benefits, although he never attended faculty meetings (Would they let him?).

He had missed four mortgage payments and the value of his home had plummeted along with everyone else's. Side jobs were disappearing as people focused on mere surviving. Recently, he had to spend the night in his office to avoid the financial Damoclean sword poised above his nostrils. If he stayed at home in his own bed, he would just panic. Sleeping at his office allowed him to temporarily avoid the home he was losing.

Because he had lost his credit cards, he had no back-up money. When not staying in his office, he was forced to spend most of the time in his apartment. He couldn't afford to drink. In the last two months he had lost about twenty pounds. Part of this was due to not drinking, but the other reason was that he had developed a chronic fixation on porn stars on the Internet. There were hundreds of them, all available in free clips and all perfectly lovely and willing. These were not the overly hirsute mons of yesteryear pornography whose pubes resembled small badgers. No. All of these contemporary women and men were shaven to smoothness. Every fantasy he had as a boy sneaking into the Minute Market to ogle the girls in *Oui*—these fantasies were now right there catalogued on: www.allyourporninoneplace.com.

Since Dr. Ford Harris was quite embarrassed about his addiction, he remained inside and equilibrated numerous times a day. He was still young enough, forty-six, and found that he just couldn't keep up with the sheer number of girls. There were highly organized catalogues with headings like:

Teen
Army
Natural Boobs
MILF
Bondage
Peeing
Czech
Blonde
Insertions (Strange)

This last one never failed to amuse him, as if all the others weren't strange. At first he began to write down his favorite stars, amateurs and pros, on yellow sticky notes. Then the sticky notes became so proliferated that he started keeping a notebook. The ones that caused him to ejaculate the fastest were on the page called "Favourites", employing the British spelling to make it seem less louche. However, that page had expanded into six pages.

Porn was just more honest than the duplicity of academia where the most qualified people were often forgotten. Why publishing one amateur novel was somehow better grounds for being a teacher with ten years of schooling like he had . . . was an enigma.

But that was the reality. He had actually been up for a tenured job the previous year. His department head loved him and made him feel at home, yet during the committee interview, they didn't focus on his love for teaching but his lack of publications. In the end, they hired someone with an M.A. and two books. He had an M.A. and a Ph.D.!

In a way, he was lucky. They paid him half as much to teach the same load, *but* they also couldn't ask him to do anymore because they paid so little. Therefore he was left alone. His students loved him and he loved them. But at nights he craved following something more natural in himself. School seemed rigidly Victorian to him. Classrooms were places of control. Faculty meetings were groupthink brain-washings about mundane administrivial issues. Shouldn't he be paid on an equal status as others, especially when teaching the exact same classes? A writer with fewer degrees and no teaching experience shouldn't be hired over him.

Finally, during his December break, a month long, he decided to make a change in some of his habits.

He was tired of working hard on his syllabi, staying up all night grading, and dealing with indifferent students: "Bro, I didn't know we were supposed to *read* the book."

He ceased doing passive/aggressive crossword puzzles, designed to make you anti-social and cross-eyed, forcing you to stare down at a box that was a series light puns muting the language into clichés.

Then he joined a gym and sprinted a lot, noticing his virility rise (with the help of fish oil).

Whenever he sat down at his desk and tried to write, though, he was inevitably drawn to a URL that presented naked edens at no cost. For hours, he pleasured himself. He felt good. He slept better. To a point. After a while, his eyes looked hollow and were rimmed like an insomniac raccoon, dark circles that required male eye cream products.

His winter break was filled with sleeting days that left behind endless slush and ice mixed now with salt. After about two weeks of sleeping late, working out and hiding in his home that was near foreclosure, he saw an ad for an online reviewer. He sent an email and immediately received a reply. The job paid $10 per review and all you had to do was watch pornos. He could write under a pseudonym or use no name at all.

After a few exchanges, he received an email with a link to the first film, then immediately received another email with a Critic's Form. His job was to watch the film and write a short paragraph, assigning a rating of one to five stars. He was not to rate on film quality or acting prowess or storyline but only on (this was their term) "spermability". Dr. Ford Harris was advised to watch each one "fresh", implying that his refractory period should have passed before responding to the next film.

The first movie was called *Forest Pump* about a dimwitted farm boy who has sex with all the farmers' daughters with names like Tammy Lou and Beulah May. As he started to watch, the gradual eroticism became insinuated into his hand, and then his libido subsumed him. However, the problem with the film was that, while the girls were voluptuous and willing, they sounded like screech owls when they spoke dialogue or screamed their pseudo-orgasms. Most of them had an acting range from A to A-. He would grow very close to climax when the director of the film would insert a completely superfluous scene filled with ridiculous intercourse:

"Hi Billy."

"Hi Tammy."

"You a-helpin' with the hay?"

"Yeah, I'm a-helpin' a-cause my daddy is gone to town."
[slices off his overall straps with a Bowie knife]
"Lemme see if we cain't help yew."
[falls to knees]

Porn had accidental humor. Bad scripts, bad actors, bad actresses but a healthy sense of play nonetheless. Dr. Ford Harris wondered why it was so taboo. He remembered that, as a child, seeing a naked woman was something beatific. After baseball practice he always bought a Pepsi and a cinnamon bun and peeked into the magazines on the stand until the clerk eyeballed him into Christian shame.

In some of the cities he visited as a boy, he recalled XXX movie theaters, but those slowly disappeared right around the Internet surge. Also, filmmaking was no longer cost-prohibitive and any dimwit with a Sony handheld could film his latest fellatio, upload it on a website and start charging. Porn stars, to him, had once been hairy, often homely and associated mostly with the 1970s. But nowadays, there was always some new, exquisite nineteen-year-old girl from around the world. His list of them was endless, whereas those quondam porn stars from his childhood seemed so few in number. Even "natural boobs" were relegated to an exotic category because most of the female stars were now plasticized walking silicon experiments.

Another question that vexed him was one that involved his personal happiness. Why had he spent so much of his life in libraries, his head bowed in silent reading like a monk condemned to prayer?

Had he missed something?

And furthermore, why was it wrong to like porn so much? It was *everywhere*, yet everyone still relegated it to the margin. But naked bodies frolicking on film: what could be more natural? Maybe that was it. Academia represented the stalwart embodiment of reason, while films about the act of sex relegated that reason back to the primitive. A woman, for example, could have time off for her pregnancy, but if you complimented a colleague of the opposite sex, it was this hysteria around harassment. The pregnancy is from a sexual act, you nitwits! Some people even filmed their children's gruesome births. It just made no sense. In Sweden men got time off for paternity leave.

If someone at the university found out that he was writing porn reviews, his career would end immediately, not that he had much of one anyway. His first review looked like this:

> *Forest Pump*, whilst on the surface a potentially excellent source of dehiscent pleasure, does not come close to realizing that bursting potential. Tammy's legendary stupidity and Billy's inability to deliver a line of dialogue combine to give us something that should be threshed *in* a combine. It is amazing how the aphrodisiac of intelligence is lost here, making us swoon more over the strapping horses in the background, their black shafts dangling and glistening.
>
> RATING: 1 porn star (for the horse).

Before he emailed his review, he signed it: "Jacques Cacque, Porn Critic".

Thinking he would be quickly fired, he was therefore surprised to see requests for five more films in his inbox the next morning. He would receive $10 checks for each film, all separately mailed from the same place. Why they did not wait and send him just one was a mystery.

By the time June rolled around and his job at the school ended, he was reviewing about seven to ten films a day. It became a bit of a hassle (and embarrassment) to constantly cash checks at his bank from PORN AGAIN, but it would be his first summer of employment where he didn't have to worry about his money ending like so many other summers of hunger and worry.

His reviews were honest and vitriolic to the core but always somewhat humorous. If he felt something, he wrote it. And each time, he feared this honesty would lead to his axing, but his invisible boss continued to send him the film links and checks.

Dr. Ford Harris kept up his reviewing and icing his sore penis. To assess the spermability with any integrity, he needed to always be fresh. And to be fresh, he had to a) drink a lot of protein supplements, b) use lots of petroleum jelly and c) work out more at the gym.

By September, he realized he hadn't even thought about applying for fall adjunct work at another college.

October rolled around and he was still at home watching pornos, reviewing them and receiving his checks.

He soon became famous for being the only critic whose reviews were grammatically correct. Porn stars, male and female, wanted to meet him. He even attended award shows and was often asked to present Johnsons, the trophy equivalent to the Oscar. In fact, he received a Johnson of his own for porn analysis. The acting in films grew better because of his criticisms.

It also turned out that the "play" he had inferred from films was not play at all. These people really thought of themselves as actors. Several of the male porn stars claimed to be gay and said that pretending to have an erection and climax with a gross woman was the highest thespian challenge. The trailer-raised female stars complained of yeast infections, jaw seizures and sore anuses. Most of them said they were high all the time and did it for the money so that they would never have to live in trailers again. It made one wonder a lot about trailers.

One evening, he was watching *Brass Nuts* about a mentally insane general and his female attaché. The review was due in a few hours. He suddenly received an email from Brandy Svetlenakova, one of the stars whom he had reviewed recently from another film.

They had exchanged cards during a porn convention. In her note, she said she found his reviews "secksie" and that she wanted to "meat" him. Her orthography notwithstanding, he half-wondered if "meating" involved something new in the industry. He decided to finish his work, write the review (2 porn stars) and then return her note.

In a few days he met her for coffee at his local café, a rather conservative spot of bald bankers and their anorectic wives jactitating on cell phones. When Brandy entered, she nearly caused a barrista to rip the handle of his espresso machine. First, she wore a fluffy overcoat that was lemon yellow, so xanthous and bright that it was like having mustard squeezed in one's eyes. She saw him and ran over and gave him four kisses, two on each cheek. They were bobbing their heads back and forth and nearly headbutting each other.

Several of the bankers eyeballed her and many of the women scoffed at her. Unlike many of her porn colleagues, she was mostly natural. Removing her yellow coat, she revealed a body of ess curves. She wore no bra and her jeans were tight as panty hose.

Many of the onlookers knew him from town, but *she* was a stranger, one that made them all feel their mediocrity instantly. Her body spoke of life, not years wasted in cubicles. The bankers didn't want people like her to be around them because it ruined their sense of purpose, plummeting egos into the averageness they wanted to ignore.

He had gotten there early and found a table for them. "Can I get you a drink?"

"Oh yesh."

Here, he noticed that her jaw was wired shut.

"I'm sorry? Can you drink with your—"

For a second she stuck her fingers up in her mouth and rooted them around her teeth. Then she removed some sort of wire apparatus/mouthpiece.

"That's better."

"What's it for?"

"Oh, for blew jobs. I give like thirty a day!"

"Oh."

"Keeps the jaw working."

"Well," he said, "I'm glad you wrote."

"Me too."

"What can I get you? You keep our seats."

"Tall mocha, please."

While standing in line, he glanced back over at her and she winked at him. He ordered and waited and returned with the two cups of froth.

As he was re-seating himself, she threw out a very unexpected question: "So, Mr. Critic, do you think that sex can one day end up as love?"

"Um, sorry?"

"Well, I got into this business because I loved all da cock. Loooooooooooooooooooooooooove it. Now I see that even feeling good can become mundane."

He was surprised by her acuity, given her prior spelling travesties and pronunciation of "blew jobs".

"It's a good question."

"Well . . . ?"

"Well, what?"

"Do you think it can lead to love?" she repeated.

"Hard to say," he replied, robotically. "I don't think anything really *leads* to love. It's sort of like an impulse buy, buying an expensive watch you don't need—you have the money, you walk in and get it, not planning on it, then you're wearing it and wondering, Why did I buy this? Love is similar to that."

She focused on stirring her mocha.

"I don't really understand a word you're saying," she almost whispered.

"Sorry."

"No, I find this feeling of stupidity to be very erotic."

How did this person who could not pronounce the most basic words speak in such a manner?

As if she had read his thought, she said, "You're probably wondering about the way I talk?"

"Yes, it is a bit perplexing. Sometimes you sound like you're three, sometimes like a philosopher."

"Well, my English is not so good, but I read very much to make it better. My spelling is still terrible."

"Ah," he said, nodding. "You read."

"Yes, I read Pushkin."

"Good lord, you read Pushkin?!"

"Yes, I feel *Onegin* is the best Russian poem."

He nodded with professorial verve.

"And would you like to make porno with me?"

This segue was rather abrupt, he thought. He tried to remain cool. "Well, I'm really a reviewer, not a—"

"I think you should make one if you are going to be such a big reviewer man. Plus I want to touch your cock with my fingers."

He contemplated her challenge but said nothing.

Was this porn star truly coming on to him in public?

The sad thing was that he felt absolutely unaroused.

Very methodically in his mind, he began to pick her apart, finding the little things to tear her down so that he would not fall for her and let her be in control.

She was embarrassing.

Too flamboyant.

No class either.

And she kept asking him about love after meeting him for three minutes.

What had happened to liking a girl first then sending her a note or sending the news through a boyhood emissary? What about "going with" a girl and first kissing her then being rebuffed for going too far then going too far and being rebuffed again but going too far even after that, slogging around the sexual bases at a crawl. Now you snapped your fingers and, kaboom, you were having sex.

He had never gotten the girls that he wanted when he was younger.

Now, those same girls were women and he could get them but didn't want them.

Endless unfairness in love, jobs.

He was about to stand up when a local friend accosted the two of them.

"Man, I've seen all your films. Your earlier work . . ."

As the fan droned on about her oeuvre, Dr. Ford Harris felt more lonely at this moment than any other in his life, so lonely in fact that he could not even conjure up another lonely moment that even compared to the depth of this one, and this heaviness cut him all around his body like a razor slicing at him, opening painful little gashes, those cuts that stung the worst, and this loneliness bled from him in these small cuts as he became disgusted with everything and just decided to leave the café.

He walked through the door and stepped onto the sidewalk and headed to his apartment, the same walk he had done so many times, alone, and now he was just ashamed that he had actually anticipated some sort of connection with her, that he had pretended they might end up together.

As he turned the corner at the fire station's endless flashing yellow light, he heard a noise and he kept going, at first ignoring it as he did so many noises, but it persisted, so he turned to see her trotting toward him, her body bouncing beyond itself.

Amazed that she could even run, he was intrigued enough to stop and see what she wanted.

She caught up with him and was panting so hard that she braced herself on her knees and proceeded to exgurgitate her mocha all over the sidewalk, the chocolate bile spreading all around their feet like blood from the head of a soldier in a movie.

He bent over with her, suspended in the moment, a barely alive wasp being spun around in the filaments coming from a spider's mouth.

"Are you all right?" he said.

She collapsed to the ground, just missing the mess and told him that she had just wanted to be with him, that she had looked forward to meeting him this whole time, that he was a snob, that he was judgmental, that he was embarrassed to be in public with her, that she thought she had something to give him, that she wanted to give it, that it was just a small feeling, yes, but it was something, right, it was something, wasn't it something?

As she spoke, Dr. Ford Harris thought of all the excuses he could use to get out away from this insane porn star. But the more she spoke, the more her false layers vanished, blankets of stupidity that she herself even admitted she had and did not want, and it was through this talking that he felt himself being touched by her, for as he was trying to peel her layers, she was simultaneously tossing them off, and soon they were oddly naked, his pretense fading also, her clownish façade gone with nothing but the gruesome chocolate oozing down the sidewalk and their inevitable propinquity and his realization that he had never even read Pushkin.

THANK YOU, SON

Harold Reed woke up one morning gazing at a maze floating inches from his eyes, a labyrinth of words and squares and numbers that had to be some sort of human error or hallucination. He had not been sleeping well at all, recently somnambulating down the stairs at 3 a.m. one morning to eat raw sausages from the fridge that were supposed to be for breakfast. Surprised that he hadn't contracted trichinosis, he did have nasty diarrhea for the whole day and made frequent trips to the men's room, where he stayed in the stall doing crosswords.

A bad night of food poisoning can really make you contemplate yourself, he wrote to himself at his computer. At his mundane work that day, the odd reverie continued, words and squares in three dimensions dancing around his eyes like geometric pixies, only to disappear the minute he grabbed at them.

A co-worker spotted him clutching at the air and, like all of his petrified colleagues, simply walked past him with a quick glance of judgment, hoping to immediately tell someone about how weird Harold was acting.

He came back to himself and stared at his computer screen, checking emails, doing research, all of it adding up to what? An office job where nine hours a day of his life consumed his time, time that now contained nothing.

What was this job? How could somebody do it every day and end up ten years later discovering that, aside from being able to pay his bills, nothing much else had happened?

He wasn't even a manager. Maybe that was a good thing. Managers tended to be people who had a healthy relationship with nothing, sticking with the same thing and becoming elevated in stature, and yet at the core they were extolled because they blissfully ignored that their lives were *really* nothing (albeit the apex of nothing). They had spent more time doing nothing and were rewarded for that time. Even paid more. They went around telling the lesser nothing-doers what to do. Their sheer time commitment to nothing had made them well-paid and respected. For *what*, Harold thought. Because you are better at nothing than I am.

This was as close to an epiphany that Harold thought he would ever come. Then again, it was an epiphany about, um, *nothing*.

The labyrinth of cubicles, the little squares of numbered cubicles themselves—he felt he lived in a maze.

He was number 41 on the first floor.

During his breaks, he would stay inside and walk through the office, starting at 1 and counting up to 64.

The cubicles were squeezed together with only the occasional empty space, and unlike other offices, if someone had a bigger spot, it tended to be the same width as Harold's, just much, much longer.

In fact, all of the bigger offices were long.

One morning, he grabbed his tape measure and decided to measure the cubicles during his morning break.

He found that number 1 was exactly 6 x 6 feet, as was number 2, all the way up to 13.

But in the second row, he noticed that number 14 was 24 x 6, as was 15.

And 16 was 30 x 6.

Every once in awhile, an office was realllllly long. Like number 20 which was 84 x 6!!! This was an important person who never came to work, and he had an office the shape of a bowling alley.

But there was order.

He was sure of it.

They were all 6 feet wide, no matter what.

Only the lengths changed.

Harold had become obsessed with these dimensions around Christmas time, a lonely vacation that he spent by himself because he didn't really enjoy family gatherings anymore. Every obscure relative seemed false and strange, second cousins who often came up to him and called him "Howard". He missed his son. His son was a kind boy.

So he stayed at the office that holiday with his tape measure and sure enough, on the first floor, the cubicles possessed a certain satisfying arrangement and symmetry.

For example, number 53 on the other side of the floor was also 84 x 6. Another bowling alley. It was the exact same length as the other one.

He was on to something.

He began to diagram his findings.

He learned a few things.

1, 2, 3, 4 (4 x 6) were the same shape as 64 (4 x 6). He found lots of such similarities, but he could still find no overall order.

This was just the first floor.

He made general sketches to keep a record of what he found.

He went upstairs to the second floor and turned on the retina-anesthetizing fluorescent light. He stood on a chair in one of the cubicles and, getting an aerial view, noticed a completely different sectioning. Since he knew downstairs so well, he walked over to number 1. Whereas number 1, downstairs, was 6 x 6, it was 30 x 6 here.

He had to be sure, and he left.

At home he opened the fridge, ate some cold cheddar cheese bites right off the hunk and drank cranberry juice from the plastic bottle. He searched his utility closet and located what he needed and headed back to the office, driving through back roads because there was no rush.

Snow had been pushed by the plows to the sides of the streets. A very large crow flew in front of him, almost staring at Harold. He liked driving alone with no particular place to be. It was a good feeling to know that he could disappear at will and go anywhere, end up anywhere, and there would always be new humans to welcome him, people whom he would probably also end up ignoring during the holidays.

Because he was nocturnal as well, he never understood why nobody in the office seemed to like the night. It was the best time to work, the most quiet, and there was an absence of dangerous traffic. Plus, the morning, that time when you were hitting your snooze button—*that* was the best time to sleep. The world was backwards.

But then again if everyone was nocturnal, he wouldn't have all the darkness to himself.

He parked and grabbed the drill and opened the door by sliding through his security card.

He trotted up the stairs to the second floor again and walked through the maze of cubicles back to number 1. Then he got under the desk and proceeded to drill directly underneath it. The bit was as wide as a half dollar.

Once he ripped through the carpet, he found the cheap floor and the drill didn't take long to find the other side. In some places there were air ducts, but, here, it just went straight through the floor. He only needed one hole that he could patch right back again.

On his knees, he placed his eyeball at the hole. It was hard to see anything. After setting down the drill on the desk, he wiped his hands and headed down the stairs.

He went to number 1 on the first floor.

And what do you know, right above the desk was the hole he had drilled.

He ran back up stairs and drilled every 6 feet of the long number 1 upstairs office.

Then back downstairs.

He noticed something.

Downstairs went this way:

1, 2, 3, 4

Each was 6 x 6.

The holes in the ceiling of the upstairs offices were above these cubicles downstairs:

1

14

17

20

23

1 downstairs met with 1 upstairs in the corner. This was clear.

He continued to drill holes upstairs and come check his findings downstairs. Over a period of nine hours, he was able to learn that every cubicle below was somehow connected to the one above it. He knew it all along! This seeming convoluted maze of nothingness was ordered. And not only ordered but rigidly so. He became so excited by what he learned that he ran to his desk and sat and tried to finish his sketches.

Perhaps it was hunger or obsession that caused him to see the visions again. He didn't know. But the numbers and squares floated in front of him. He had made hundreds of holes in the floor and when he turned off the downstairs lights, the glow from upstairs shone through each hole like a star of its own. Beautiful lights beamed through the myriad holes and he worked in this soft luminescence, architecting a chart to explain it all. He became famished and toiled through the night, seeing the visions whenever he looked in front of him. If he looked down at the sketches, he was okay.

It must have been four in the morning when he stared at the ceiling and the light beams shining through the hundreds of drilled holes, when he finally saw them. The holes weren't holes at all.

They had become letters, single letters that formed across the ceiling. He began to run around the first floor writing them down and comparing his sketches to the order above him.

Was it a message?

He didn't know.

It was right there.

What was this?

And then it came to him when he saw the section of a newspaper folded on a desk. A crossword puzzle. He had been working in a crossword puzzle for the last ten years. Right inside one. That explained everything. The cubicles, the organization, the way people walked through this maze each day like robots. Letters formed through the holes above each cubicle.

How had the holes turned to letters?

How would he fix all the holes and make the floor look like new?

He completed the puzzle eventually and searched for clues.

He drew a 15 x 15 grid and filled in what he found. But as he began to make sense of each word, 1 across, 5 across, etc., he noticed that while he had discovered a completely perfect puzzle, the across clues in the first floor cubicles, the down clues in the second floor cubicles, the actual letters and words they formed were meaningless. Even when he mapped the across onto the down, all the letters were gobbledy-gook.

It was this point that he decided to quit his job. He grabbed his drill, left the holes open and headed home with the visions worse than ever. Only now, instead of just being right in front of him, they were all over the place, in the snow drifts, in the sky, filling his car. He swatted at the squares and numbers and words like annoying gnats.

■   ■   ■

After the holidays, he decided to visit the manager one day and talk of his visions and his malaise. Right after the break, the manager had dropped by Harold's cubicle and presented him with a new number 41, a sticker that Harold was free to paste up himself.

He didn't *want* a new sticker.

His boss was all bothered by the holes in the floor and was still trying to figure out the culprit. It took Harold a long time to have the courage to see him, but he finally did, taking his drill with him.

Maybe he would confess and get it off his conscience.

He knocked on the long cubicle.

His boss was all the way at the other end.

"Come on in, Harold," he said.

Harold walked down the bowling alley, not knowing what he wanted to say. He felt a screw in his pocket, a long one, and pulled it out to examine.

Who lives a life of death, becoming a man who doesn't feel except to yell at someone in traffic or to be annoyed by a co-worker chewing with his mouth open as he eats out of a white box of Chinese food?

He didn't need to contemplate dying because he was not alive in the first place.

There were no high places nor were there any lows. Just a long life in the middle, a flatline like a dead man in a hospital, flatlined but alive somehow.

And yet alive for what?

He had money. He could have gone to Africa!

Why didn't he?

Why did he choose to fill up his days with death as he lived?

What could he do to change the fact?

There was no worse fate than turning cold. A cold person was somehow wrong, existing certainly but for wrong reasons. His antipathy was buried and brutal and silent. It lurked in the cave of himself, hidden beneath layers of stone, a sleeping chimera that never wanted to be disturbed.

The letters filled the puzzle in front of him. His work was the across part of a puzzle where he spent time each day, and above him was the down sections.

Wherever he looked, there were squares and rectangles: rooms, computer screens, parking lots, tennis courts, crossword puzzles, newspapers, tables, desks. Order everywhere masking the coldness. Perimeters containing numb things and numb people.

"What can I do ya for?"

"Nothing."

"Why do you have drill, buddy?"

The battery was charged and he just wanted to see if he could drive something into his boss's head.

Would the screw turn easily into the man's brain?

Harold stared at his boss for a long time.

Suddenly, he was squeezing the face of his boss with two hands, trying to push his cheeks together.

Then he leaned forward and French kissed the man, his tongue swirling around, a child on a water slide.

The drill was on the desk.

He stopped kissing his boss.

He tilted back his head.

It was amusing to look up and still see all the holes in the ceiling.

His boss was wiping his mouth in disgust and trying to call security with his other hand.

Harold felt like a horse sleeping standing up. It had been a long time since he had felt right.

"Never mind," he said to his boss. "I'm leaving."

"Why did you kiss me?!"

Harold thought he was sleepwalking.

He went back to his desk, grabbed his keys and drove home, wishing that he could live inside the snow.

Soon he was driving in it, sliding around in a field of white.

It blurs here for all of us.

Harold is in the car, sliding, then the car can't move.

He is out of the car.

White blinds him.

He is sitting now, back against a tree.

A crow lands on him, on his foot. The clumsy black bird pecks on the red trickling from the bottom of his leg. It seems to be drinking it.

Harold prays for a vision. He knows he's emptying. What he doesn't know is where he is. The puzzles are puzzling.

It blurs more.

His son finds him.

Harold is taken home.

His son has done this often and aches to see a man fading, a little worse each time.

Harold will be back.

He will leave again.

He doesn't want to be alone. Just ends up that way and there's not much to do.

One is across.

One down.

But his son has found him again.

Thank you, son.

KING OF THE TREADMILL

I am the King of the Treadmill. Look at that woman on her cell phone. No phones in here! Yeah, keep talking on it even though you know I'm watching. Rude.

And, you, orange-tan growth-hormone guy. Stop dropping the weight plates for maximum noise levels. We get the point: you are a strong doofus with a small weewee. Are teeth *supposed* to be the color of snow? Your orange-tan friends aren't helping you look any smarter either.

Oh, thanks over there, thanks for the headphones so loud I can hear them twenty feet away. I'm happy to listen to music I hate. No, really.

And shut up downstairs in the spin class—that is not exercise. The Treadmill is the only true training.

Hey, I'm looking forward to seeing your varicose balls in the steam room. Seriously, it's my favorite time of the workout.

Uh oh, look at this one. Is that Botox or did someone zap your eyelids with a taser? Jesus, woman, you're ninety, let it go. Oh my god, this must be her sister from the circus.

How about this guy? Wow. Is that a walnut in your tights? You smuggling in a robin's egg? Lovely visual.

I have the biggest, most toned quads in here. Let's take a second to examine them in one of the many mirrors available to me in this physique mecca.

I'm looking around. The Treadmill is right in the middle like the trombone in a symphony, the closest sound to the human voice. I am the King. This is MY gym.

Wait—oh, oh—I've seen this young couple before. The super hot model chick avec the faux boobery alongside the balding milquetoast who is so plain that everybody asks, "Why is the super hot model chick with *that* guy?"

Only two hours to go.

I'm only supposed to be on here for thirty minutes, max, and I know there's a line, but I need to get in my two-and-a-half hours, so you can keep staring, honey! I'm not getting off here anytime soon. I also heard you on your phone earlier, so paybacks are a beaaatch, beaaatch.

Hey, why is that the most out-of-shape people at this place are . . . the trainers?!

Uh oh, psycho anorexic ex-girlfriend at five o'clock. Yikes. Man, she looks unhealthy. Don't come say hi, don't shame me, no, no, oh, hey, hi. Good. Good, I'm good. I'll see you later. No, not right next to me. Oh, thank god. Go not eat somewhere else. Anorexia. Social disease my ass. Herpes, that's a social disease.

Ooo, I'm a bad person for making fun of anorexia. Screw anorexia, screw steroid steak heads. My sister had anorexia. In the hospital she would run in place by her bed like a crazy skeleton to lose weight. Our father had to buy her two new teeth because she vomited so much that the acid burned them away. So don't talk to me about anorexia.

I hate this place, but that's why I am the King of it. I rise above the hate and internalize it and kill you in my head, and then I don't have to beat you with my fists. It's basically the Christian ethic— but with weights. A silent gymnasium insurrection.

I remember my first time on the Treadmill. I put it on level 15 incline. I glided upward, my legs pushed like a locomotive, and I could keep going forever, an infinite series of steps that gave me the feeling of constantly ascending yet remaining in the same place.

This is my domain.

I am tired of Thomas Jefferson doing some creative writing and acting like people are equal. Some are better. It is a fact because I am one of them. In the gym all are *un*equal.

Who else can ride the Treadmill for close to three hours!

Nobody.

That's why I am the King!

I'm not pumped; I'm toned. *Natural.* Not artificial and empty like these . . . that woman over there pisses me off, always on her phone, talking loud, GET OFF YOUR PHONE. Read. The. Signs. Damn soccer moms. Aren't they supposed to be *teaching* manners not distorting all notions of propriety?

A few weeks ago, I started CLABS, Club Abs, for people like me with really great abdominal structure. Yes, I'm naturally blessed, but I also work hard and eat a diet of mostly protein shakes and vegetables. I'm not averse to puking up food when necessary. Anyway, I'm cut. Ripped is a better word. CLABS is for folks with similar superior stomach muscles. We do not allow in FLABS (Flabby Abs). So far, no one has joined but a guy named Fernando. I should also see my doctor about CRABS (no acronym).

To be truly fit, you have to be alone all the time. Even when I'm resting, I cannot stand proximity to people. Girls used to be fun. Now they're just talkative and terrible. I used to have crushes all the time; however, I think those were due to too much sugar cereal as a boy. I don't have crushes anymore, in any case. But I also stopped eating sugar cereal. Hmmm.

Wait, wait, here he comes, the finance guy on his phone talking about a deal, ooooo, an important deal that needs to be discussed at the auditory level of a pterodactyl. Economy crippler! And yes, your wine gut makes you appear to be in the second trimester.

God I hate the gym, if you want to know the honest truth. It's a terrible place, an experiment by nerd scientists somewhere turning us into monotonous, exercising rats.

They are studying us, I'm pretty sure of it. Rise up against yourselves. The establishment is not your friend!

Now this guy. *This* guy. I can't stand him. Yeah you. Fantastic, hang out right in front of the sign that says CELL PHONES PROHIBITED and talk as loud as you can. You jail reject. Aren't you late for a skin-cancer appointment in your local tanning bed? Go drink a smoothie or something. You don't scare me. What? Do something about it. Wait. Are you coming toward me? Go away. Oh nice, here he comes.

Meatface with Missing Neck: Hey was dat boderin you?

Toned King [Me]: Yes.

Meatface with Missing Neck [more aggressive]: I mean, was dat like really boderin you?

Toned King [Me]: Well, yeah, you're pretty loud.

Meatface with Missing Neck [threatening]: I can back it up too.

Toned King [Me]: [Silently making okay sign with fingers and thumb.]

Idiot.

Every time I work out, I search for the cameras or the one big eye staring down at me. I'm sure some of the scientists studying this place are right here among us, maybe even next to me on another Treadmill. Maybe that Meatface was a scientist, testing me.

But I know I am the best white rat with red eyes in here. I am the rat with the best abs on earth.

POOL MAN:
A Reality Story

"'God hath given you one face, and you
make yourselves another.'"

Hamlet, III.i

Who Is Pool Man? ♀ ♂

I am Pool Man, but I was once a pool boy too. The truth is that I stopped having time to clean pools. At a certain point in my dazzling career, I outsourced all the pH checking and leaf vacuuming to the teenagers, the young pool boys. It was good money for them and it freed me to take care of the women.

I have a deep attraction to women over forty-two.

I like facelifts and fake everything.

I enjoy wrinkles, cellulite and lines around the eyes.

These things signify wisdom in a lady and I prefer that to anything else.

However, you could say that I am complex because I am fond of facial reconstruction.

Perfecting the body is much like finding the right balance in a pool. I'm sure they use logarithms in calculating components of plastic surgery, just as pH is nothing but a logarithm of the reciprocal of hydrogen ion concentration (in grams per liter). No wonder we have an affinity for each other.

When it comes down to it, I like to think of myself as philosophically shallow, on the other side of the rope from the deep end.

On the surface, I may seem a man who cleans your pool with that vacuum robot, but I know a good facelift when I see one.

I once knew two women who would give each other Botox injections in the restroom of a fancy divorcee pick-up bar. One night, they were drunk and sniffing a little too much Mr. Snow when one of them jammed the needle right in the middle of her friend's pupil. I rescued this woman by pulling out the needle and rushing her to the emergency room. Strangely enough, her vision actually got better in the "damaged" eye.

My story is a simple one, slightly chlorinated and full of intentional metaphors about water.

Is it better to be submerged in a pool and be unconscious?

Or to sit beside it in an uncomfortable chair as the sun burns you?

Or to avoid the pool altogether and go inside for a drink or two with the housewives?

I usually ended up doing the third.

The Basics of Pooling Herewith Exposed

As with any art, you need to know the essentials of the discipline; there is no circumventing the basics.

On your truck you need:

1) A long pole
2) A vacuum head
3) A hose
4) Chlorine tabs
5) Four bottles of muriatic acid
6) A garbage bucket
7) Your lunch
8) A test kit
9) A brush
10) A stop log of customers
11) The leaf master
12) Some marijuana (personal use)

A daily routine consists of between ten and twenty stops. Wednesday is usually the day for once-a-week accounts.

A typical routine goes something like this:

1) Grab all your stuff
2) Pray there are no dogs
3) Test chlorine and pH first
4) Empty skimmer baskets and pump baskets (watch for snakes on this one!)
5) Backwash pool filter
6) Skim pool surface (my personal favorite)
7) Vacuum
8) Brush sides
9) Add chemicals
10) Leave
11) Contemplate pool

In addition, there are the Ten Rules of Pool Man:

1) You are required to be submissive, gracious and humble at all times to all women while also being some odd blend of cowboy, dog, and shepherd.
2) You must never say no to a woman.
3) You must know the difference between the sundry types of female orgasms.
4) You must understand all facets of balance.
5) You may be with many women simultaneously but you must pay attention to each of them individually.
6) A mansion usually has one lonely woman in it.
7) Do not laugh at plastic surgery.
8) Do not make fun of shopping. It is like dating for married women.
9) Pay for dinner (unless she is a dominatrix).

10) If there is a husband involved and you find yourself falling for the wife, then you need to prepare for the fight.

And finally, there are two scientific corollaries to pooling. They are quite simple:

1) If the pH is too high, add acid or sodium bicarbonate.
2) If the pH is too low, add soda ash.

When I was younger, I preferred being outside and checking pH. At one point, I wanted to be a glaciologist and to study ice formations, but glaciers are a lonely business. Later, I felt the need to be indoors. Indoor pools were not the same, but they were a good compromise.

When I was mentoring, I sometimes watched a younger pool boy from a bedroom window and reflected with nostalgia on the time when I skimmed leaves from the top of the water.

How Mrs. Rabeson Caused Me to Discover
My Innate Love for Older Women

It began in the Boy Scouts when I was twelve and away from the orphanage for a while. I just couldn't figure out why the boys were hanging out with other boys most of the time. This made no sense to me. I never understood the merit badge either. Or the skill award. Or that sign with three fingers. Where are the girls, I wondered? At Boy Scout camp, we competed with each other in races and took classes like basket weaving. At night we ate carrots and potatoes cooked on a fire in aluminum packs and slept in smelly tents after eating blackened crusted marshmallows and insulting each other with hyper-pubescent tropes, such as:

– "I hope you suffocate to death inside a small mustard packet."
– "You look like frog throw-up."

–"I hope you spontaneously coagulate."

During one of these nights of occipital apathy (while smelling Josh Steiner's body odor in the tent), I decided not to hang out with the male population anymore. What, after all, did males really offer the world besides the fraternity party and bad investment banking?

The next day I went to the pool and befriended the female lifeguard in the red one-piece, Sally Beth. She worked at the camp during the summers saving money to be an osteopath, and she taught me that a good lifeguard never enters the water. I applied the same principle to becoming a master pool boy—and eventually Pool Man.

"Sally Beth," I said, in my boyish innocence. "Girls seem a lot more fun than boys."

"Oh they are."

"I love them very much."

"Well, let me tell you some secrets . . ."

Sally Beth invited me up to her home in Santa Barbara after Boy Scout camp. Although I was young at the time, I had the nervous feeling that something was about to change. As I entered the house, there was a woman waiting for us.

"This is my mother, Linda Rabeson."

"Hi, Mrs. Rabeson."

"Linda," she said, holding my left hand between her soft palms.

"Linda," I repeated, staring up into her eyes.

Since my parents had given me up as a baby and I had been an orphan all my life, I often found myself staying in random places. I ended up living at the Rabeson's house for about four months.

I had a pretty good deal with the orphanage in Los Angeles at that point because I was the only one who knew how to maintain the pool. They let me come and go as I pleased as long as I helped them. I'm also sure that was one of the reasons that I never got adopted. The head of the orphanage, Father Rick Penumo, prided himself on a clean pool and often used it as a sacred baptismal.

That first night at dinner, Linda and I could not stop talking to each other. Her dress was a scrim of angelic white.

There was no husband to be found.

"My father died when I was much younger," said Sally.

"Yes," Linda added. "He was a good man."

I felt uncomfortable as they both squeezed their lips together in that face one makes when indicating pity. It is usually accompanied by a sad tilt of the head and perhaps a bit of wistful nodding. Linda sighed and then we began to eat the meatloaf placed before us.

As I chewed my food, I contemplated this mother. While her daughter was tall and slender with long blond hair parted in the middle and sensual gap between her two front teeth, Linda looked nothing like her. She had perfect posture and hair the hue of a salted almond, reddish-brown with flecks of white. Her eyes were stoplight green and her lips stoplight red.

"So . . ." Linda said, lifting her glass of red wine and staring right at me.

"Mom, don't gawk at him so rudely."

"I'm just admiring him."

"He's twelve. Don't forget."

"Oh, who cares?"

"Please don't fight," I begged them.

"Sorry," Sally Beth said. But she was angry and threw down her napkin on the table. She backed up in her chair so abruptly that it fell backward. I came to the other side of the table and picked it up as she huffed up to her room. The gesture seemed terminatory, and she wouldn't talk to either of us for the next couple of days.

"Well, I'm sorry about her," Linda said, placing her napkin on the table.

"That's okay."

"She likes you," she added.

"She does?" I replied.

"Yes, but you don't like her like you like me, right?"

I paused.

"It's okay. Just be honest."

"Yes. That's right."

It was very true. My body was warm and I thought I was sitting next to a million toasters. There was something about the resonance of her voice that touched me, as if a ladybug had landed on the hairs of my ear and tiptoed around.

"Would you like to go see the rubber tree by the pool?"

I nodded. "Yes, of course I would. I've never seen a rubber tree."

"Just leave the dishes."

We stood and she grabbed my hand, the first person to really touch me in such a way. But it was not just her hands that caressed me. It was as if her eyes and her voice had small hands of their own. I felt touched inside and outside of me.

We walked through the French doors and she showed me the rubber tree, oozing thick white sap. The pool was in the shape of a carrot. She turned to face me, touching my face with both hands and then she leaned over and kissed me on the forehead, her lips lingering for just a moment.

"Would you like to stay in my bed tonight?"

"Sally Beth won't be mad?"

"She understands."

"She does?"

"Yes. Think of her as a . . . sister."

"Okay."

I held my gaze on her like a little frog staring up at its first fat fly. She taught me how easy it was to look at someone.

That evening we fell asleep together after talking through the night.

■ ■ ■

Since she had been an English teacher, Linda later introduced me to all sorts of novels, plays and poetry, and we would often sit by the pool discussing the difference between types of metaphors like the metonym and synecdoche. Or if we studied ternary feet in poetry, she was fond of such words as amphimacer (long, short, long—"Peter Pan" foot) and amphibrach (short, long, short—"romantic" foot).

Sally Beth's initial jealousy abated and she and I became friends again, often playing Monopoly with real money. The house turned into some sort of Eden for me as I managed the carrot-shaped pool.

Once a week, I called the orphanage and walked them through its own pool cleaning over the phone.

My body became a honey color under that Santa Barbara sun and I felt as if I glowed with happiness.

I slept in Linda's bed every evening and what will probably seem strange was not at all to me: she and I only touched each other and told ourselves how much we loved being together. It was an affection I had never known, one that had threatened me in previous years because of its silent power, but after just a few nights with her, I no longer feared being touched. One stroke of her fingers on my neck caused a shiver down my back.

The Annoying Roger Stuck

The months passed as if they were days. Then one of the neighbors, Roger Stuck, began snooping around the house a lot. He was a single man with the nose and eyes of a ferret and had worked behind a desk stealing people's insurance money for most of his life. His breathing was heavy and he usually had a bucket of Kentucky Fried Chicken that he carried with him in a headlock. It was not uncommon to see him gnawing on a breast in the middle of the afternoon while also watering his white roses. He never liked me very much because I think he had designs on Linda. She invited him over to the pool a little too often for my taste, and he seemed to be plotting something by the way he eyed me.

"How old are you?" he asked when we first met.

"Twelve."

He looked at Linda and shook his head. "Twelve!"

"Isn't he the cutest pool boy you've ever seen?"

"I've seen cuter."

Except for Roger, everything was bliss. Yet I was also becoming unsettled and feeling that I had overstayed my welcome. I developed a sudden desire to leave and Roger didn't help. The more Roger came over, the more hostile he became. One time, he was a little drunk on bourbon and ginger ales and so was she. They were at the pool playing Scrabble, and he could only come up with words like "gum" and "gin", while she was annihilating him with "hypoxia" (oxygen deficiency in the tissues) and "kiblah" (the point toward which Muslims pray at Mecca).

I leaned over the board. "Roger, you really are terrible at this game."

"Shut up. Go play with a toy."

"You're terribly dumb."

"Be quiet."

"Okay. I will let you concentrate on your next big word like 'fry' or 'cat'."

"Ha ha," Linda chuckled.

"That's not funny."

"He's just the most darling little boy."

She smiled at me and I winked back at her.

"You two are disgusting," Roger sputtered. "You're lucky I don't turn you in to a social worker."

"For what?" she said.

"I see what's going on," he mumbled.

"Roger, you shut your potty mouth."

"I don't have to."

"Leave her alone," I warned.

He pointed at me. "Look, you little pubic lice, I could beat your head in with my pinky toe. What you two are doing is illegal, I'm afraid."

"Why?" Linda interjected. "Just because he sleeps in my bed?"

"He does?" Roger replied, sort of gulping a little.

I felt sorry for him because I could tell that he liked her a lot. There is always one moment when a relationship turns in a different direction and this was that time for us. Relationships must progress or perish, my mentor, Funny Duck, always said. Roger shook his head and stood to leave. Linda was close to crying and I somehow knew that it was time for me to go too.

"I'm calling a social worker tomorrow," Roger said.

"Now why are you doing this?" Linda nearly screamed.

"It's not right. He's just too young."

"You're just jealous of him because you've wanted to go out with me."

"That's not true," Roger lied. "I don't think I like your non-benevolent attitude."

I forgot to mention that Roger was also a devout Christian who tended to fall into church-speak whenever he was backed into a linguistic corner.

"Roger, he has not done anything to you and we invited you over here as a friend."

"I don't care. I have to make the call and do God's work in earnest."

"Don't bother," I interrupted. "I'm leaving."

"You don't have to do that," she pleaded.

"I should. I have stayed way too long anyway."

"But—"

"Oh dear Lord," Roger said, slapping his forehead. "Why don't you date someone your age!"

"Roger! Stop it. This is ridiculous."

"Why won't you date me? What is wrong with *me*?"

"Rog," I said, "you eat a bucket of Kentucky Fried Chicken every morning."

He dropped his face into his hands and began to cry.

"I can't make anybody happy," he blubbered. "I'm sorry. I'm sorry I threatened you. I didn't mean to threaten you. I won't call the social worker. She's right. I was jealous. I have to go and pray to my Jesus statue."

He stood and went through the house and that's the last time I saw him.

But something had changed between Linda and me. She knew that she couldn't keep me there for too long. I had been seduced by the privacy that she and I shared and, hence, had forgotten about my age.

I wanted both to leave and to remain with her.

We talked for five hours into the night and by morning our eyes were dry from crying. Sally Beth had been away with her boyfriend. They drove me to the station and I watched Linda Rabeson and her daughter grow smaller as the train pulled away from Santa Barbara.

I thought about *pool* in that moment and how uncentered I became when away from it. A lake is dirty and its filth covers all the bad things. But a pool is clean and nothing can hide in one for long. The pool is a moving truth, if you will, a body of sincerity. Diving into pool water is like disappearing into something true. I did it only once and because it was necessary. I'll tell you about that later, though. That dive was like becoming a young god washed by the water, surfacing wet and cleansed. I was never the same after it.

Los Angeles: The Formative Years

Funny Duck was my teacher, master of the craft of pooling. He had a mafia connection at the orphanage and was able to get me out of there finally when the time came. But I did come back there for a bit after leaving Linda. He was a real jarhead from the Marines and his head was a tall rectangle with a perfect flattop, the hair of which resembled a mown lawn. He was also a bit of a mythomaniac who told me that he could do things like make pasta out of his underarm sweat.

"I learned it in Haiti."

"Gross."

"Not if you use onion powder."

He also tormented small children at the orphanage pool about his strange theories.

"Every night, you die in your sleep," he would say to some poor four-year-old. "And you might not come back."

". . . I die every night?"

"That is correct, soldier."

"Waaaah."

Funny Duck was a sly fox, albeit one that had narrowly escaped a major fender injury by bumping his head only slightly on the front bumper. He often vacillated between enmity and irritability.

On the hottest afternoons, he mowed the lawns around the pool naked, except for his combat boots with black socks.

At night, he slept in a self-contained glass tube in the pool house. He truly was a harbinger of early pool ideas that he had culled from his military time in China and Japan, where he learned much about Confucius, the Tao and other philosophies of the Far East.

One afternoon at the orphanage, Funny Duck had seen me scooping out a perfectly shaped piece of defecation from the pool. He watched me for a while, then he took me to lunch and explained the situation.

The pool, he said, is just an idea behind everything else. "In fact," he added, "it's the place that hides us."

"I follow you."

"You do?"

"I think."

"That's a relief. You have the makings of a great pool boy. Would you ever consider making it a career?"

"Possibly."

He stared at me.

"What?" I said, a little uncomfortable.

"The ladies."

"What ladies?"

"You have to know how to deal with the women."

Here is where I learned to become an entrepreneurial vessel of pleasure.

"This is all about commerce of the body," Funny Duck told me. "If you do it right, you have to exist in a moral and philosophical state of vacuous non-being."

He sneezed about four times in a row from his reefer allergies.

"Okay," I said, wondering exactly what he meant.

"You heard about exploding toads?" he asked.

"No."

"Toads can just blow up. It happens."

"What does it mean?"

"It means that you can explode too."

"Meaning . . . ?"

"Too many questions. Let's get to work."

He would often drop such puzzling koans on me, meant to push my thoughts beyond normal ways of viewing things.

The first house where he took me was the home of a famous Russian actress on a mini-series who later mothered the child of Alfred Hitchcock's nephew.

It was in Bel Air and the pool was the size of a lake.

I had explained my rule about not entering the water to Funny Duck. And he understood.

He set me up at the back with a pair of pink rubber gloves and a long white scooper net. There were party streamers throughout the pool that were purple, green, and yellow. I had to remove them. Funny Duck had gone inside.

As I found the motion, my mind became clear and I disappeared to a quiet trance. I had once read that a trance is Latin for *passage* and originally meant the state of passage from life into death. I often fell into a similar state when cleaning a pool.

I guess about an hour passed before the Russian actress appeared at the patio door.

I could tell right away that she was forty-three.

She smoked a small cigar and wore an orange bikini.

Her skin had never seen the sun and was like glass painted with white paint.

Her augmentations were sublime.

Her Botox was Michelangelo-like.

Her facelift cuts were barely noticeable.

Her lips were pulled back like a fish on a hook being dragged through the water.

The pool was now clean and a pile of streamers sat by the diving board like soggy spaghetti.

"Where's Funny Duck?" I asked her, and put down my scooper.

"He's gone."

The smell of her small cigar floated over to me.

There is an eleventh rule of Pool Man, my own, and it states that the best moments are unspoken. As she stood there and stared at me under her dark glasses, I waited and then I finished my job by going inside for "a glass of lemonade".

After awhile there was not much competition for me in Los Angeles since most of the pool guys had been in the sun too long and smoked copious pot.

Funny Duck helped me make my way through various subdivisions of Santa Monica, Venice, Hermosa, and Manhattan Beach.

For five years, the money flowed into me and I placed it into an account that grew exponentially.

I spent until age twenty under Funny Duck's tutelage.

It was right around the time of one of my last pooling lessons with Funny Duck that a razor close call occurred. He never ceased to have some theory about the pool.

I often took notes on a pad, not because I wanted to but because he made me.

"First," he lectured me, "most women cheat on their husbands. It might be flirting or sex or even shopping, but women cheat and they do it very well. Second, women know that men are dumb and that they will never usually figure out things. Third, dumb men are just so happy to be with someone *besides* themselves that they convince themselves everything is fine."

He paused and stared directly at me, which was unnerving, adding:

"But why do you think the men built pools in the first place? They constructed them because the pool is an unconscious representation of all the cheating that goes on without their knowledge. Most men never swim in the pools either. They simply want them in the backyard as a reminder."

"And how does this information supposedly help me, Funny Duck?"

"You'll find out soon enough," he continued. "Write this down. In truth, the pool is a symbol that a woman can leave a man anytime she wants. The men *know* but they drown it in the clean water. Underline that last part. They also know that a pool cannot exist without a pool boy. And they don't really mind pool boys because most of them are harmless potheads. However, every once in awhile someone like us comes into the picture, and it is here where every fear rises to the surface. We are Pool Men for a reason."

"I still don't quite get it."

He breathed in deeply, trying not to grow impatient. "Let me give a little history about the pool, son."

"Sounds good. Because I'm entirely baffled."

"I believe that God is very much like pool water," he told me. "When I clean a pool, I am cleaning God. And I try to pay regard to God at all times, even when I'm committing perpetual adultery. You should too. 'Pool' is a polysemous word and its multiple meanings somehow converge in spite of the differences. For example, a pool is a small body of water. But it is also a game of chance, a lottery of sorts. In addition, it means 'to gather together'. And of course, it is a game played with green felt and pockets and colored balls. How can one word mean so many things? Water? Lottery? Gathering together? Game with sticks? Because the pool is a place that contains all meaning."

"Interesting," I agreed, nodding.

"'Pool' also derives from the Old French word 'poule' meaning 'young chicken'. And 'poule' is a derogatory word for a loose lady. Thus, even within the word itself is implied a certain lifestyle between men and women."

"I think I'm getting it," I said.

"Oh. And stay detached at all times," Funny Duck reminded me. "Never get close to anyone."

The close call came the next day.

The woman was forty-five and she was an actress on a sit-com who had mothered a child by Ronald Reagan.

The husband, however, considered himself a swinger and liked to talk to me all the time while I worked at the pool. He also stayed at home way too much. Plus, he wore a silk robe that "fell" open "accidentally" all the time.

I just do not like to talk and that is one of the virtues of a good pool boy. In fact, people who talk too much tend to be lonely, psychotic or on television.

His name was Roger (yes, another Roger) and his wife openly treated him with casual disrespect. Roger had made a fortune in the toothpick business by adding onion flavor to them. It was a fad that failed in the United States but, for some reason, became very popular in Thailand.

There was a faint smell of onion and wood throughout their mansion. Highly phallic sculptures of bronze toothpicks stood in the front yard, as if unexploded rocket bombs had shot up the place.

Funny Duck, at this point, merely came by to collect money for my services and to pay me my cut. With all the wireless technology, I rarely saw him and he was able to send my money directly to my Cayman Islands account every week.

Therefore I was left to having a discussion with Roger, the open-robed toothpick magnate.

"So . . ."

He could never remember my name.

"Moon Tiger," I said, making up a new name for myself.

"Moon Tiger! Right. How's the pool looking?"

I turned to him. This very mundane type of questioning was typical of most owners of their pools when they had the opportunity to consult with the pool boy himself.

"Well," I informed him, "it's off-balance."

"Really?" he said, retying his robe.

"Yeah, I think someone urinated in it."

"Seriously?" he nearly yelled.

I held up the pH to him. "There are also amphetamines in here."

"Ocean animals! What the hell are they doing in a pool?"

"Amphetamines," I corrected him.

"Thought you said amphibians. Sorry. My bad."

"This is some kind of speed."

I examined the vial.

"Oh, that. Yeah, I pour that in there for parties."

I nodded.

Now, keep in mind that his wife was upstairs in the bedroom

waiting for me. I had seen her open the curtain a few times and look.

The toothpick husband would not stop talking to me, though. It was trouble waiting to happen because she had paid Funny Duck earlier and I knew I couldn't leave the house until I had done my job.

"How long you been cleaning pools, Moon Tiger?"

"All my life."

"Yeah."

He leaned his head to me.

We were up in the Hollywood Hills and a traffic helicopter passed right before our eyes, almost on the same level as the house like a giant wasp from a movie.

"Damn helicopters," he said.

The noise passed and it was quiet again.

He nudged me with a playful elbow. "Hey, you want to go to a concert at the Viper Room?"

"No thanks," I demurred.

"You sure? It's a band called the Bagged Maggots."

"Sounds fun but I can't," I demurred, growing impatient.

"Too bad. I'm meeting a friend there you would like. He's a designer tampon salesman in Orange County."

I had nothing to say to him on this matter.

It was a recipe for social ridiculousness.

In my head I thought, "If this is time and that is your hands, you have entirely too much of the former on the latter."

"You want a shot of gin?"

"No thanks."

"You sure?"

"I'm sure."

"Positive?"

"Yes," I said, gritting my teeth.

He strolled to the outside bar and poured himself a shot of Tanqueray.

He shot it back.

Then he poured another one.

He gulped it back also.

"Did you know that the Queen Mum, before she died, used to drink two glasses of gin a day? Two *glasses*. Not gin and tonics. *Glasses*..."

His monologue droned in the air like an electric toothbrush.

I moved into a Zen frame of mind and etched several mental haikus, logopictographs I liked to call them.

"Look," I said, politely as I could. "I have to floss pretty bad and should probably, you know, *do* that."

"No problem, man. No *prob*lem."

He backed away from me with his hands lifted behind his head.

Forgetting he still held the shot glass, he dropped it behind him and it fell on the concrete, not breaking.

Then he stepped on it as he backed up and fell, his robe untying itself on the way down.

Later, he stayed inside watching t.v. and reading a paper. The afternoon improved a little bit, sort of like when cold hard cheese finally melts on a piece of toast.

I cleaned the pool, checked the pH, and even scrubbed the blood off the diving board (some head injury at the last party).

Finally, I walked inside and decided to risk it. Roger lay on the sofa taking a nap, his robe wide open with his flaccid penis hanging down like a jalapeno pepper.

I strolled past him, walked up the stairs, found her room. I had noticed myself growing closer to her.

I was no longer detached.

We fell into each other.

She kept calling me "her little sweet honey baby".

When I turned, I saw the husband at the foot of the bed looming over me, breathing heavily through his nostrils.

He loosened the silk belt of his robe and let it fall to the ground. He walked toward the bed and knelt on it, then crawled over to us.

She stared at him.

"Excuse me," I said. "Bathroom."

I hustled to the toilet and found a window and nearly defenestrated myself to death.

Luckily, there was a small roof where I landed.

I scaled down a gutter that nearly ripped from the house.

It was time to leave L.A.

How I Came East and Lost the Girl

Throughout my driving trip across the country, I could not lose the smell of chlorine on my body. It stayed in my nose at all times.

Funny Duck had pointed me to the suburbs of Manhattan to Greenwich, Connecticut.

He said there were a lot of pools there.

When I finally drove into town, I was famished. I found a tavern restaurant and ate by myself. A very pale waitress with platinum hair came over to me.

There were no words and I prolonged my meal by ordering multiple drinks and extra appetizers.

I was conscious of my chlorine smell when I signed the credit card bill and left the restaurant.

Outside, she smoked a cigarette.

"Hello," she said.

I waved without speaking.

"I saw you in there," she added.

I nodded. Her cigarette smoke floated away like a cartoon bubble of words she couldn't say. I watched the smoke and thought of the sound of a pool, small waves that never have the chance to grow bigger.

Pool waves are safe and create little splashes. A small wind can stir a pool to life and give it movement without really disquieting it.

This new girl was like a pool after a small wind. On the surface she was calm but had intense eyes.

"What is that smell?"

She kept sniffing.

"Probably chlorine."

"You been swimming?"

"No. I don't swim."

"Why do you smell like chlorine?"

"I'm a pool boy. Studying to be a Pool Man."

She nodded and smiled a little. It was a cruelly humid June evening and I had just pulled into Greenwich in my blue Porsche 911. I had driven all the way from Los Angeles, only stopping for gas and convenience store peanuts, which have a low glycemic level.

As we stood outside the restaurant, I noticed a Metro-North train whoosh by us. She finished her cigarette and dropped it to the sidewalk, pressing it with the toe of her expensive red shoe.

It was dark and I had to find a place to rest. Funny Duck had given me the number of a man for work, but I was not ready to plunge directly into business. I needed time away from the pool, yet I had to be near it.

A dilemma.

At such moments, mistakes are usually made. If you compromise yourself at any point, you are certain to end up in a bad situation, scratching your head and asking how you got yourself into the mess.

I knew no one and she seemed to like me.

For the first time, I actually looked at her face.

I kept staring and then figured out the issue: she had a facelift. Suddenly, I was not only attracted to her but mildly jealous. She was so young though. Why would she ever need to alter her face?

I leaned closer and realized that I had touched her cheek with the back of my hand, not out of affection but attempting to locate the lines of surgery. None. Perfect incisions.

"What are you doing?"

She opened her mouth and took my finger all the way in it.

"Um," I said, "could I ask you a personal question?"

"Sure?" she tried to say while sucking my finger.

"Did you have a facelift?"

"Yes."

"May I touch it?"

"Yes."

We were soon driving in the dark through the backcountry mansions of Greenwich on North Street, massive houses that seemed to have no one living in them, castles of loneliness. The speed limit was 45 but I took the Porsche to 120 and it felt as if I were suddenly bathing in adrenalin.

Rose, the girl, couldn't keep her hands off me. I could not get over her beautiful facelift. She told me the story of her previous face as we drove. She explained to me that her earlier face was exquisite but just not her. As a child she had an idea of the kind of face she wanted and even though the one she had was extremely attractive, it was not a true reflection of *her*.

I listened to every word and believed she might have been talking about my own face.

I liked my face. Many liked it too.

But it never was a fit.

I, too, had an idea of how I wanted to look.

I dreamed of getting my own facelift one day.

We talked a bit more about shampoo products and facial toners and then I floored the pedal.

We hit 125 and she pointed to a turn that I must have taken at 100.

She flew out of the car.

I couldn't find her.

I combed the whole area with a flashlight from the glove box. At one point, I thought she might not have been real. She was nowhere to be found. It didn't change the fact that it was hot and dark and that I was on some side street in a posh neighborhood in the middle of the night. I thought it best to stay in my car and see if she returned to me. No luck.

I fell asleep at the wheel.

When I was awoken with that stale feeling of driving too long, I was not on a street but parked right in front of a house worth millions. It was the most grotesque piece of sybaritic architecture I had ever witnessed.

There is sharp aroma of chlorine that enters the nose so suddenly that it tickles the nostrils, not dissimilar to a bouquet of wine. I could suddenly smell the pool. I also detected an essence of oak, jasmine, roses, even blueberries.

After a little bit of triangulation on a small pad of paper, I calculated that there were no less than forty-six pools in the purlieus of North Street Greenwich. I inhaled numerous times until I had a sense of the place.

Then I headed into town and went shopping.

All morning, I visited Ratleigh's on Greenwich Avenue, where I purchased many facial products, including a cutting edge ear lotion, specifically for the lobes.

"It's made of ostrich sperm," the shoplady informed me. "And it's good for your micropigments."

"Ostrich sperm?" I doublechecked.

"Yes," she said with such boredom that she reminded me of a horse that had fallen asleep standing. Nevertheless, she was very kind to me and I decided that I would be a regular customer. I even purchased a $7,000 woman's fur made from frog cilia that could be worn stylishly during the summer for a "winter look".

After I bought my coat, I put it on and went to the blush counter, manned by a stout German whose fingers were as thick as the fat end of carrots. I surrendered to her application of several blushes on my face. She was dressed like a Swedish stewardess with a red neck scarf. When she spoke, it was as if some stentorian general had taught her the art of maquillage: "YOU APPLY IT HERE. UNT HERE!"

My face disappeared in the red and peach and raspberry blushes and under her large hands. I thought tears of affection might drip out of my eyes for her.

As I closed my eyes, I dreamed of a day where men everywhere could walk into women's stores and not feel the prejudice against purchasing man products. Man products have been created for men *by* men, yet the majority of males know nothing about them.

For example, did you realize that there is an actual product made specifically for the Adam's apple? It is a white cream that moisturizes the larynx from the exterior, permeating the skin through a process known as Collagen Seepinage. That's just one prime example. Another is the Incan clay cream loaf facial aloe sputum splash with oatmeal that is made by expectorating pygmies. Not to be forgotten is an eyeball toner that apparently cleans the pupils much like Windex (but with organic ingredients). I prayed for men all over to be exposed to these age-reducing efficacies. When I opened my eyes, I saw all the shopladies surrounding me and smiling.

An Intervening Carnal Episode

I checked into a Spanish style hotel on the water of Long Island Sound.

After I unpacked my few belongings, I decided to walk up the street for a facial, a manicure, a massage, a pedicure and an espresso, in no particular order.

Upon buying my espresso (the adult beverage that separates us from the animals), I found a shop run by Korean women whose indecipherable chatter hypnotized me as my toes and fingers awakened under their touches.

I leaned back my head and rested and reflected on my personal religion about pools. The facial felt as if a layer of my skin had been peeled off.

Later, back in the hotel, I put on my characteristic Pool Man outfit: jeans shorts and nothing else but a faded red bandana wrapped around my neck and a brown Stetson hat. This "uniform" is recognized as the universally distinctive clothing for pool boys and men throughout most of North America.

I found my way to the pool, meandering through the maze of the hotel and smiling at people as I passed them.

Oh, and I also wore black flip-flops that clacked on my heels as I walked.

By the pool, I saw her in mirror aviator glasses and a white bikini.

She was forty-three.

One-hundred percent plastic she was, and I loved her.

Her tan was so orange that I thought she was an orange at first.

I sat right beside her and noticed that there was truly nothing real about her.

The fake is the real now anyway.

I stared at her and she was equally intrigued by me.

"So," she began, "what do you do?"

"I am Pool Man."

"A pool man?"

"With the capital P and M, yes."

She picked up a pack of cheap cigarettes, pulled out one and flamed it with her neon yellow lighter. The smoke hovered for a bit, and then a small breeze carried it a few chairs over to a couple of senior citizen men who waved the toxin away as if it were nuclear miasma.

The sun melted me and I returned her stare.

When she was down to the last bit of the cigarette, she put it out on her arm and the skin sizzled like a fried egg in an oily pan. My eyes widened at this gesture, but I wasn't surprised. I had seen worse.

She wanted to walk up Greenwich Avenue. When we were nearly at the top of the hilly street, she found a ladder on the side of a building and we scaled it in semi-broad daylight.

I watched her calves shimmer in front of me and noticed a million moles all over her legs and back, an optical infinity of dots.

We were now on the roof and she simply walked over to the side and got on her back and peeled down her bikini bottoms so that they were just pulled off and wrapped around her orange thighs.

Her wrist bled where she had put out the cigarette.

Her pubic symphosis and my seminal vesicles were in concert. My prepuce, frenulum and corona touched her A-spot on the way to crashing into the cervix. My corpus spongiosum and Cowper's glands glissaded off my prostate as the bottom of my stomach rubbed her mons veneris. My corpora cavernosa filled with more and more blood and I became firmer and firmer and the small mouth of my meatus opened and . . . I was sliding away from myself and disappearing into her and I had a vision that had never come to me before that moment.

The two o's in pool were almost like eyes staring at me.

I was swimming through the water while wondering why I never swam.

It was sublime congress and I bathed in this melody of woman.

After it was done, she pulled up her bikini bottoms and asked me if I wanted to grab dessert somewhere.

I said sure and we climbed back down the ladder and found an upscale restaurant that she seemed to have visited more than once. In fact, several waiters and bartenders came up to her and hugged her, kissed her, spun her around. One man even lifted her up on him and she wrapped her legs around his waist as he performed a few exotic dance moves. She tilted back her head and her brown straight hair dangled and nearly touched the floor as she leaned back. I watched all of these interludes and decided it was not worth waiting for her, and I turned to leave.

She noticed that I was going and stopped me.

"Sorry about that," she said, grabbing my hand.

We sat in a blue booth and she ordered a Lollipop Tree. When this dessert appeared, most of the dining room turned to stare at us. It looked like something that escaped from the equivalent of the insane asylum for desserts. First, several suckers had been stuffed into the "trunk" of the tree cake and on the end of each stick were cheesecake balls covered with chocolate. The frosting appeared to be made of bubble gum.

She handed me a fork and I took a bite. It tasted like someone had burned sugar in a rotten pumpkin. I grimaced and placed the fork on the pristine white tablecloth.

I had a chance to stare at her face and noticed her teeth that had been whitened. I asked her about her dentist and how the procedure had gone.

"It was all right. My teeth ached for a few days."

At that moment, I wished that I were a superhero, Pool Man, who, by holding his breath, could turn into a small pool and escape all teeth conversations. I was done with her and excused myself to the restroom, except that I ended up leaving the restaurant altogether and running down to the water, back to my hotel.

The Biggest Pool Ever Built

I went out later for a waffle and eggs.

After my meal, I found a pay phone.

Funny Duck had given me the number of the home that would become my central place of pooling. I put gas in my car and asked the clerk at the convenience store about the address. He looked at the piece of paper and eyed me.

"That's the biggest mansion on North Street," he said.

I thanked him and jumped in my Porsche and found my way back to the same place where I had lost that girl. And wouldn't you know: the house was the exact same one that I had slept near just a night earlier.

I picked up the phone at the gate and informed them who I was.

I was about to speak in more detail when the black iron gate rolled back to the left.

I drove the car up a driveway made of silver bricks. The house was big but in the sort of way that a shopping mall might afflate out a smaller version of itself. It was also five stories high with extremely progressive post-modern architecture that caused it to look like a cross between a hospital, a red barn—and a schooner boat.

The white porcelain robot of a woman who opened the door to the house was the maid from Sweden.

She wore a nametag that said, "Mengta."

I nodded politely and asked if The Van Williams were home.

"Dey are at the bowling alley," she said, with the dryness of hot sand.

"Ah," I replied, saddened that her career as a comic had never been realized.

"Dey *own* da bowling alley."

"I'm sure."

The following pause filled the room with so much silence that I became anxious and nervous as a new lamb walking.

"Who you?" she said, eliding the verb.

"Pool Man."

"Pool Man! Come. Come on me in."

Her English, though incomprehensible, had a certain charm to it.

She practically yanked my hand and escorted me through this modern castle filled with an overabundance of bright green and yellow furniture.

"We been waiting for you."

"Really?"

"Yes, Funny Duck a friend of you?"

"Yes."

"Well, Funny Duck, um, helping us a lot."

"So where's the pool?" I asked.

We walked to a window that seemed almost the color of chlorine itself. I loved that windshield wiper fluid look. The window spanned hundreds of feet to the ceiling.

"There," she said, pointing to the very window where I gazed.

"Where?"

"You looking at it."

Then it hit me. The entire wall was a glass side of the pool, the biggest one I had seen.

And I had seen many.

My mouth fell open in awe and I thought I might have just met my match.

To access it, we had climbed five-hundred stairs. At the top I felt as if I were staring over an ocean of a pool.

There was no backyard, only a pool that went sixty-feet deep.

It was as high as the house.

In fact, we had exited on the roof in order to see the *size* of the pool. It was commodious and seemingly infinite. At that moment, I had arrived close to a form of satori, a Zen epiphany I often tried to achieve during yoga class. The Swedish maid smiled at me. This was nearly the greatest honor I had known.

The First Dinner with the Family and How I Handled My Interview for the Job with Aplomb

The bigger the pool, the deeper the problems.

At dinner that evening, I met four people at the table:

1) the father, a movie producer
2) the loud and buxom mother

3) their alcoholic son
4) the young wife of the son

Imagine my surprise when I discovered that the young wife was Rose, the girl I had lost from the car earlier!

All of them lived in the house and barely talked to one another, but they convened at dinner every night as if it were some sort of business meeting about the purchase of paper clips.

In fact, the first dinner was my interview.

The father's tan skin reminded me of some sort of Gila monster and his white hair was parted in a perfect line on the side. His pink scalp appeared to glow moistly under the whiteness like a sunbathing worm.

His wife had a head the shape of a globe and she chewed with her mouth open throughout the meal. At certain moments, pieces of masticated corn fell back onto her plate, but she didn't notice and scooped up the chewed food with the remaining meal and ate it again.

The table was something out of a Dracula movie where one person sits on one side and the other person sits a mile apart. However, we were clustered at one end and rather close in our throne chairs carved from wood with gargoyles on the tops.

The young woman, the very recent bride of the son, seemed to have fallen into a tub of peroxide. Her lily-white skin and towhead hair glowed in radiant albino incandescence.

The young man was prematurely balding with hairs sprouting from his head like a recently hatched chick from an egg—but a chick that resembled Winston Churchill. He had a thin face and spoke using that Connecticut jaw jut, coolly apathetic and terminally submissive. While everyone else ate roast beef, corn, and potatoes, he scooped spoonful after spoonful of Beerios into his mouth.

What was so impressive about his eating was that he had no bowl. He had simply cut open the yellow box on its side and had poured the can of beer directly in*to* the box, after which he had dropped about six tablespoons of sugar onto the cereal. And he had inherited his mother's genetic ability to chew in loud smacking chomps.

As I answered questions and watched this Petri dish of odd culture, I wondered when I could actually go to the pool, not just look at it.

"So," said the father, who was English. "I make films."

"Really?"

"Yeah. They're monolithic scrotum secretions."

"Why's that?"

"They're shite."

"Any reason . . . ?"

"Lots."

He pointed his fork at me for emphasis.

"For example, actresses with no talent. Second, actors with no talent. Third, everybody gets paid too much for making bad things. Fourth, movies aren't art. Fifth, the public is stupid and fat and addicted to junk food."

"Now honey," the wife interrupted. "Your movies are bad but they make money."

"That's right, Dad," the son said, a Cheerio falling off his bottom lip, landing on the table and rolling like an errant tire down a street.

"Pick up that Cheerio, you stupid git!" the father yelled.

"Eff you," the son replied.

At this point, Rose began to ask me questions. "You have wonderful skin," she said to me.

"Thank you," I replied, trying to see if she remembered me. She did not seem to recall me; I thought it best not to bring up the subject. I told her about various toners and creams I used.

The mother, father, and son stared at our hushed conversation with mild interest.

"Think you can handle that pool out there?" the father challenged me, pointing over his shoulder with his thumb.

I smiled.

I didn't even have to answer but I did. "The pool falls somewhere between honor and duty for me. I try to honor my past teachers by paying homage to the pool every day. I often meditate on the word *pool* and place myself in a state of what Carl Jung would call 'active imagination'. It is somewhere within a dream but balanced by a vigorous sense of reality. That is why the pool comforts me."

The family now gazed at me with furrowed foreheads and widened eyes. I could have easily been a naked midget with six nipples, but I often noticed this reaction when I spoke about the symbols of a pool. I decided it would be best to stop speaking and chew my roast beef.

"Well," the son said, finishing his Beerios and now pouring himself a glass of red wine. "You certainly have thought about the pool a lot."

"Yes, I have," I told him proudly.

The mother tilted her head to examine me in a different way. "I like your theories."

"Me too," said the father. "Let's give you a trial run. You can live in the pool apartment and eat with us here every night. Our personal chef was once a Croatian slave who had been brainwashed during some war. We found out about him in a catalogue. He makes a devastating shrimp bisque that's dairy-free. Dev-astating."

As the meal continued, I went over all the anagrams of "pool" in my head. Loop. Polo. Ploo. Lopo. It was a form of linguistic contemplation that I often utilized during dinners with insane people.

After eating dinner, we drank apple dessert wine and ate brie cheese, except for the son who now had twelve blueberry Pop-Tarts in a stack on a plate. He poured syrup over them and cut them like they were waffles.

The Unsinkable Tony Moroni

The next morning, I awoke to the grandeur of Pool. Somehow, it was calm as silence and there wasn't the slightest undulation of water.

I thought to myself about what Funny Duck had promised them.

I imagined that I would now be caught in an intricate, dramatic snare of human behavior and tried to assess what my supernumerary carnal duties could possibly be.

That would come later.

Now was my time with this beautiful, beautiful pool.

For the first hour, I sat on the ground with one hand in front of my face and stared through my fingers at the pool. I called this particular ritual: Feeling the Water without Feeling It.

As I worked at my casual pace, Rose walked around the pool and came up to me. "Do you like our pool chairs?" she said, indicating the purple furniture in the shape of trapezoids.

"So those are chairs?" I said, squinting.

She began to inform me that they were environmentally safe and made from already chewed grape chewing gum.

"Each one cost five-thousand dollars."

"Who chews all the gum?"

She shrugged. "Not sure. Probably poor people in the Philippines?"

Her dour face glowed under dazzling peroxide vividness and she stared at me with curious intent. Her eyes seemed to indicate some secret we shared, but if there some clandestine message, it was *very* secret because I had no idea what it was. I could only assume that her recent marriage had caused her some labial dismay and she simply needed to someone to listen to her.

"How big is this pool?" I asked.

"Three million gallons," she replied, trying to remember the datum. "I think."

"Hm. That's hefty."

I visored my eyes with my hand in the bright sun.

A silence descended on us like a large graceful bird too awkward to fly in the right way. The wings flapped and the bird landed at our feet, struggling to stand as it spun around itself.

I wanted to concentrate on the pool, but my other job had already begun.

She winked at me and formed her lips into a kiss. I nearly leaned over to place my mouth on hers.

"Oh, by the way," she said, suddenly remembering. "You have an assistant."

"I do?"

"Yes," she said. "His name is Tony."

"Where is he?"

"In that cave."

She pointed.

"Er . . . cave?"

"If you walk to the other side of the pool, there are some man-made caves. He lives in one of them."

"Tony?"

"Tony Moroni. We got him from the Organic Homeless Shelter."

"There's an Organic Homeless Shelter?"

"Yes," she informed me. "It's all vegan."

At that moment, the father came outside with a video camera and held it closely on our conversation. "Keep talking!" he yelled. "This is amazing."

"Um . . ." I said, trying not to be conscious of the camera. "Is Tony a trained pool man?"

"Hah!" she guffawed. "I doubt it."

I looked toward the cave area right when a man emerged with an eye patch, a bald head, and a beard down to his stomach. He wore red women's heels and his hirsute legs were so hairy that he appeared to be wearing swatches of carpet.

"There's Tony now."

The father directed the camera toward my new amanuensis. Tony smoked a pipe and also wore an orange life vest for some reason. He walked self-consciously down the side of the pool and approached me.

"You the new pool man?" he asked, looking at me intensely with his one visible eye.

"Yes, I am Pool Man," I said, emphasizing the majuscule letters.

"I see." He nodded.

The father now brought the camera so close to Tony's head that the lens almost touched his face.

"You trying to blind me!?" he shouted, and backed away with his fists up and ready for a fight.

"Oh, calm down, Tony," the father said. "Or we'll send you back to the shelter."

"Shit, that place is nicer than this prison. At least their food is organic and they don't waste styrofoam."

I could tell that Tony had probably been hired as a pool boy but could not deliver the proper services.

"I'm gay," Tony admitted. "Let's just get it out."

"Okay," I said.

"Don't hassle me."

"I was going to congratulate you."

"Cinema verité!" screamed the father, moving his camera around in all kinds of haphazard motions.

"Why do I feel like I'm in a warm bag here?" Tony said.

"Don't have a kitten," the father said.

"Tony's lover is a small Chinese man who lives in the cave," the young wife told me.

"Manku," Tony announced, proudly, "is asleep right now."

"Well," I said, "we don't want to wake him."

"No," Tony said. "We don't."

My Television Reality Show

The father often followed me into his own bedroom and taped me with his wife. This bout of open-mindedness was indeed refreshing. In the middle of certain acts, he would come over to me and give me directions, as if we were actually filming a movie.

"Hey, can you just look back at the camera every once in a while?"

"Sure."

"Good, good."

He backed away.

"More energy. Think of cotton candy. Cotton candy."

His wife looked at her watch. "Honey, can't he and I just have a little time alone?"

"In a bit, babe. Right now I need you to imagine being inside blue cotton candy. That's important for your actor's arc."

"My what?"

"Your arc."

"I didn't realize I had an arc."

"You have an arc. Every actor has an arc."

"Can I fake an arc?"

"No!"

"Why not?" I asked.

"Because. Your arc is in you and it finds you."

"Ah. I see."

"Good. Cotton candy. Arc. Bear them in mind."

He was a serious particularizer when it came to these directions. One time he told me to "envision a grilled cheese sandwich" and when I asked why, he quickly changed his mind and said, "No, scratch that. Think of a short sheep with only two legs . . . but peeing."

■ ■ ■

The indolent son fared much worse and drank a lot from the moment I arrived. I had to be more secretive with his young wife, Rose, although the fellow seemed to know that his inadequacies fueled my need for balancing them. I would take his sweet little wife out to dinners, concerts and picnics, and she would boldly refuse protection.

At one point, we were at a party in Manhattan and she and drank at least twelve vodka tonics. People were spanking one another with frozen fish sticks.

My albino mistress resembled an etiolated aloe vera plant, bleached from lack of sunlight.

Suddenly, we left the party in a vapor of alcohol. Outside, she pulled me into an alley and she pulled me into her. Right afterward, she straightened down her skirt.

"I'll find a way home," she said, "*if* I go home."

"You sure?"

"My husband is a drag."

She pulled out of her purse a small version of a bicycle tire pump. There was a needle on the end that she stuck right in her bottom lip, proceeding to pump it up with collagen. I watched the lip expand like cookie dough being squeezed through a piece of plastic. She could barely enunciate her words after this procedure and we said our temporary farewells.

I hopped a train in Grand Central and was on a Metro-North train to Connecticut.

I had been to the city in a tux and was now on my way back to the succor of suburban Greenwich.

I was on the last train, the famous 1:30 a.m. Vomit Comet, and I fell into napping and dreaming of Linda Rabeson.

Father's Day Inspires an Idea

Back at the mansion Father's Day was in full force and we all ate at the big table, including Tony and Manku.

It was here that the father announced his new idea to follow me around Greenwich on my various Pool Man trips, tape them, and sell them as a reality show.

No one mentioned that the young wife was still not home. The father said that some people were already interested in buying my show and that we needed to get busy, at which point the son broached his concept.

"I have this idea."

"You?" the father challenged him. "An idea? I doubt it."

"Seriously."

"How long is this story by the way?"

"Come on, Dad."

"What is it? Hurry up."

The son proceeded to explain that he wanted to make a documentary film of the father following me around.

"A documentary film about the making of a reality show about a pool man?" The father seemed impressed.

The situation was becoming more like ouroboros by the moment. The snake that eats its own tail was diminishing in size.

"But isn't this reality show a documentary itself of sorts?" I asked.

"Sure, sure," the son said. "But a documentary film about documenting a reality show. Now that is AWESOME."

They were all very proud of themselves, and I couldn't help but feel that my privacy was about to disappear.

The next morning, they woke me early.

We drove to a famous writer's house who had a nature show about figs on P.B.S.

She was short but with a full body.

She greeted me at the door as the father held the camera on us.

The son held the camera on his father filming.

Inside, she and I chatted over mimosas. It was morning, so we were both amorous, except we started to do kamikaze shots and before I knew it, she was standing at a microphone.

"Come sing Cat Stevens with me."

"Cat Stevens?"

"'LONGER BOATS ARE COMING TO WIN US, HOLD ON TO THE SHOOOORREE.'"

"How about Queen! 'PRESSURE, PRESSING DOWN ON ME. PRESSING DOWN ON ME, NO MAN HAS FALLEN, UNDER PRESSURE.'"

I went up to the other microphone she had set up and sang harmonies with her as she gulped down a pill that she said was the combination of Ecstasy and Prozac and Xanax.

"Man, this is great stuff," the father said, running around in circles to get all the angles.

"Don't eat the blue acid!!!" she screamed.

I now stood on my head singing Cat Stevens with her, the blood rushing to my brain. As I remained in this position for an hour, I nearly passed out as she pulled off my jeans.

The father put the camera on my face.

I was red, my eyeballs bulging with gravity.

Losing My Focus on Pool

When my life became more commercial, I was never alone.

I missed the solitude of vacuuming pools.

I was growing bored, not really knowing if I was being myself in front of the camera.

Would I act this way or that if the camera were not on me? I didn't know because I was too self-conscious.

The summer turned into a blurry whirlwind of appointments and filming. It seemed as if sex was now as mundane as cauliflower.

In order to keep my mind from deliquescing, I joined a book club and started visiting town council meetings. I often suggested books about pools for the all-female club, but no one ever wanted to read them.

Nevertheless, I was the only male in the group and soon the father discovered my secret avocation and began to film the book club.

To make matters more complicated, all of the women were over forty and had decided to form a pedagogical fellatio club *within* the book club.

By now, Manku and Tony were also holding cameras. The reality show pilot was a foremost sensation and I was asked to be on all sorts of t.v. shows.

But I was getting far from pool and needed to recenter myself.

After a twelve-hour book club orgy, I decided to make some changes in my bubble of idle privilege, mostly by eating more pickled ginger in my diet.

During a date with an actress from the book club, I spanked her with novels in a local book store. We were in the literature aisle as she expressed to me her fantasies about avisodomy (congress with birds).

Her husband happened to walk up at this time (he had been following her) and he was gnawing rapidly on a submarine sandwich as if he were a spastic sheep dog that had to ingurgitate grass for fear of starvation. He wore a black suit and a red tie, some sort of bland uniform for the financier.

"Look, you country toad, stay away from the wife."

He pointed at me threateningly with the sandwich, a layer of ham jutting from the side like a tongue from a sleeping drunk's mouth.

"*The* wife?"

"You're just a pool guy."

"Just a pool guy?"

Did he know who I was?

"She told me about you. I didn't think you would push this far."

"Well, can she talk too?"

"Not right now," he replied.

"Why not?"

"Honey," she said, grabbing his arm.

"Quiet dear. I'll take care of this." He flung her arm off and took another bite of his meal.

I yawned, glanced at my watch, and folded my arms. He came very close to me, his nose almost touching mine. Mashed bits of ham and bread were smeared in the gaps of his teeth. You can tell a lot about a person by the way he chews. His forehead did not just sweat but oozed a thick secretion like French soft cheese. His patterned baldness must have started in his college days when some of his fraternity brothers began pulling it out for a hazing prank.

Finally, he finished the last morsel of his sandwich and he continued to harangue me.

People in the bookstore began to stare at us as the pitch of his voice raised a few decibels.

"I'm tired of guys like you preying on my property when I'm at the office all day."

"Property?" the wife reacted, with a hand on her hip.

"Honey, not now. Go look at some Suzanne Somers exercise books."

He came even closer. "Now, you stay away from her."

"She came on to me," I informed him.

"I don't care. You've got to respect me and leave her alone, no matter what she does. I work hard and don't think it's fair to come home to this."

"I'm afraid I can't do that," I said, backing up a bit.

"Why the hell not?"

"Well, I don't believe in marriage as you view it. In fact, I think it's an institution designed to fetter women. About a hundred years ago, women were listed as property in most county records along with the horse and the house and the saddle. That's why women took men's names. What occurred in this process, however, was that women were deemed less equal than men, but it really was the result of a few litigious, insecure men (who probably had unhappy wives cheat on them) who made the laws."

The husband cocked his head to the left and listened to me.

"Now, women still take men's names. Why? Women can vote and are seen as much more equal these days, but marriage still carries that historical memory. Is that fair to women? I don't think so. See, you're buying into a bureaucratic notion of love and you probably don't even like your wife. You see her as something to own and that's not right, now is it?"

"No, probably not," he admitted.

"There. See? You and I can be friends. I'm not trying to 'take' your wife. I just want her to be happy as a person. If you just let me do my job, then you can hold onto her without any hassles."

"Not a bad thought," he said, now crossing his arms and nodding.

"I'll bet you that your wife has been with at least four other men this month."

"Okay, how much?"

"Fifty bucks?"

"Sure," he agreed.

We shook on it.

He was not a bad fellow after all.

"Honey," he said, calling to his wife who had stepped into the exercise books aisle.

"Yes?"

"Come here for a sec."

She came over. "What?"

"How many guys you been with this month?"

She looked at me in shock.

"Go ahead," I said. "It's okay."

"But . . ."

"Don't worry," I assured her.

With a bit of trepidation, she finally said that she had been with seven men.

"This month?" the husband nearly choked, unable to believe her.

There was then a moment between the three of us, an understanding that the truth, while full of sting, is always best.

"Hey," I said, "I'll leave you two alone for a moment. I'm going to the café for a squishy muffin. Anybody want one?"

"No thanks," he said, smiling at me.

"No," she said.

He reached out and put both hands on my head and said, "You're all right."

I rode the escalator down to the café and bought my squishy muffin and returned in a few minutes. They were getting along fine now. In fact, he had started to cry.

"Hey, Rainy Face, what's wrong?" I asked.

"I don't know," he blubbered. "My life . . . it's just a sad mess. This economy is killing me."

"Come on. Let's sit down somewhere."

We found some chairs and all three of us sat together. He really broke down, waterfalls of tears that flowed out of him beyond his control. His body shook and the wife stared at me to do something.

"I'm not in love with anything or anybody," he began. "My job is a void. All this time I put in and when I finish a day, I have nothing but more money. I haven't painted or written or raised a child. I have absolutely nothing to show for my time. I am wasting my life completely. Look at me. I am out of shape. I'm ugly. I've turned into this grotesque fool."

I smiled and began to tell him about the array of male facial products available to him, and he seemed to effervesce like champagne at the thought of cleansing his pores and using moisturizer on daily basis.

"You need to take some steps," I instructed him.

"Like . . ."

"First, you have to stop wearing suits."

"Okay."

"Then quit your job."

"Okay."

"Stop screwing your sixteen-year-old nannies."

"But—"

"Ahh—" I interrupted.

"Okay, okay," he acquiesced.

"Give your wife the freedom you give yourself."

"Okay."

"Don't eat meat for twelve days."

"Okay."

"And try to see me as an ally. I am on your side. Your wife is much happier after she's been with me. Otherwise, she would sue you so hard that you would have little attorneys growing inside you."

His tears had stopped by now and he stood. She and I stood with him and he hugged me, hard. He would not let go.

"One last thing," I said into his ear.

"Yes?"

"You need to finally start dating men."

"I know."

"Just for a little while and then you can date women again if you want."

The final moment was a bit awkward.

He wanted to stay, but in the end I had to tell him to leave us alone.

Not before I gave him a piece of paper with a recommended psychology book about soul. "Go buy this and go home."

"Okay," he said, sheepishly.

"Take care," his wife said. "I'll see you at home later."

He waved to us both.

"Thanks again," he said to me.

"You're welcome," I replied, and went back to spanking the wife's derriere with a book of monologues, as she bent over for me and explained her fetish for statues, also known as agalmatophilia.

I Want to Be a Recluse

By now I was in demand everywhere and needed a sabbatical. Back at dinner that evening, I told the menagerie that I needed a break.

"A break?" the father nearly choked. "No way."

The mother continued chewing on some pork and her gums flapped like a maniacal goose.

The son was happier than ever because of the documentary, although he and his young wife were not speaking much.

Apparently they wanted to have a child but he was not able to get her pregnant.

She sat by me at the table all the time and she usually sneaked into my room at nights.

"I'm just a bit tired."

"We have twelve shows to deliver," the father said.

"We?" I responded. "I didn't sign anything."

"Doesn't matter. You want to live here, then you have to do this."

"No I don't," I told him, rising. "Please don't tell me what to do."

"Relax," he said.

I rethought my plan to punch his nose, remembering how he had become cellularly unglued upon seeing four Colombians mowing his lawn at the wrong grass height. He actually lassoed them with a rope and swung the four of them around until they all fell down in a state of dizziness. I had watched this situation from the window of my pool apartment.

Tony and Manku arrived late and sat down, luckily defusing a potential conflagration between Pops and me.

The son finally spoke: "Look, I'm almost finished my documentary. I just need a few more days of footage."

He was so affable about the whole thing that I relented, sat down, and simply requested a few days of respite.

The father agreed and said we could film more when I returned.

I said that I would feel more refreshed in a few days and would be able to give them the shows they needed.

I Find Out Some News, Twice

I was putting back on my shirt after frissive delectation with the chewing-challenged mother.

"I have to tell you something," she said.

"Shoot."

"It's a bit strange. I'm not quite sure how it happened."

"What?"

"Brace yourself."

"Okay."

"I'm pregnant."

The first reaction of Pool Man in such a situation should be utter aplomb and complimentary kowtowing.

"That's wonderful," I said, and leaned over to kiss her. "I'm extremely happy for you."

"I'm fifty-four-years old."

"Oh?"

"It's your child."

"Hm."

I nodded and thought for a moment.

"You should absolutely have it," I said.

"Are you kidding?"

"Not at all."

"I can't have it, Pool Man. Can I?"

"Have your husband film it. This is great stuff."

"You wouldn't mind?"

"No," I told her. "I have several children all over the place."

"You do?"

"Yes," I affirmed.

"And do you support them?"

"Spiritually, sure."

"What about money, though?"

"I send them all money."

"That's good."

"How many do you have?"

"I don't know. Eleven?"

"Eleven!"

"Twelve?" I re-guessed.

In any case she and I worked out the situation in an amicable way. I went to bed that night realizing that I needed to do a tally of my kids at some point. One should always know how many children one has.

As I mulled over this calculation, my door creaked and the young daughter-in-law entered in black panties and no top. She had the libido of a frenetic rabbit and she shuddered the very second that her smooth skin touched my clean sheets. I kissed her and we began our gambol. She often whispered fantasies into my ear and tonight was no exception: "I want a small man, nine inches tall, to come in my nose."

I'll have to admit that I was a bit taken aback by that one, but I encouraged her. Always entertain every fantasy, Funny Duck once told me. We moved in the bed for hours and her pliant body was warm as the fresh milk of a goat.

Afterward, she usually left to go back to the bed with her snoring husband.

That night, however, she turned on the lamp and light filled the room.

She sat up and pulled her knees to her chest. With her arms

folded over her knees, she began to whimper and tears fell from her eyes in large drops.

"What's wrong?" I said.

"I don't know," she said, crying fully now.

"You sure?"

"What's our deal?"

"You know our deal," I told her, falling to the floor and doing some Marine clap pushups.

"I feel as if I like you, though. This pretense is silly. Everyone knows about us, but you never seem to show any feeling toward me."

"Of course I do." I had done five pushups already.

"Sexual feeling maybe. Otherwise, you are distant and abstract."

"Isn't that what you want me to be?" Ten.

"Not always. You can't spend this much time with a person and not grow closer to them."

"I can. Hang on. Let me just do twenty-five."

"How? Emotions are supposed to accrete. Can you stop doing those damn pushups!"

"One sec."

I finished and hopped back on the bed, breathing heavily.

"You really are something," she said. "You can't even talk to me."

"Talking gets people into trouble. Talking typically signifies a need to fix something that is unfixable."

"Look, I know that you are unavailable. I just want to *talk* about it. I don't want to change that aspect of you."

"Um," I said. "Okay. Hey, do you think my pecs are too huge?"

"Too huge? No. They're fine."

"All right," I said.

"I didn't mean to break down like this. I'm sorry. We had an agreement."

"Yes," I reminded her. "We did."

"There's something else."

"What's that?"

"I'm pregnant."

"Gulp."

My eyes widened as I remembered her mother telling me the same thing just that same day.

The first reaction of Pool Man in such a situation should be utter aplomb and complimentary kowtowing.

"That's wonderful," I said, and leaned over to kiss her. "I'm extremely happy for you."

On My Day Off I Make a Bad Choice and See Myself in a New Way

Since it was my day off, I went to my Pilates class, then to get my hair cut and re-highlighted, then to my yoga class, then to my acupuncturist, then to my deep-tissue masseuse, then to my hypnotist, then bungee-jumping, then indoor rock-climbing, then finally rollerblading at the beach at Tod's Point in Old Greenwich.

I watched the sun set over the silhouette of Manhattan in the distance across Long Island Sound.

That night, I wrote in my journal and watched several movies about swimming pools.

My favorite French film, *Swimming Pool,* was about this woman, a writer, who invented all sorts of lustful scenarios with this young blond vixen. You never knew what to believe once you realized you were in the protagonist's imagination. (Naturally, I found the older writer much more attractive than the young nymphette.)

I also watched the English film *Sexy Beast* that took place around a pool. Some very good pool cinematography in that one.

And of course who could forget the Robert Redford and Mia Farrow version of *The Great Gatsby* when Gatsby died in the pool at the end.

Then I made the egregious mistake of watching a DVD of my own reality show.

The father had burned me a copy of the shows thus far.

I opened the machine, placed on the disc and hit the CLOSE button.

It was as if my blindfold had been lifted right as all the guns were killing me in a firing range.

First, the camera work was off-putting, lots of zigzags and strange angles. I nearly developed a migraine headache just trying to figure which person I was. There were several shots of my naked bottom, which I didn't mind, but the most disturbing aspect of the filming was the lighting.

It was like walking into a diner at four in the morning and seeing nothing but painful fluorescence beaming onto some bright yellow scrambled eggs.

And I objected completely to the tone of the show.

They were clearly mocking me.

I thought it was supposed to be homage.

All these caveats notwithstanding, I could not stop watching the damn program and in fact viewed several episodes.

The next morning, my second day off, I phoned Funny Duck to tell him about my issue with the mother and the daughter-in-law.

"Yikes," he said, after listening to me.

"What should I do?"

"I imagine they'll both have them."

"That's what I figured," I said.

"And pretend the kids are the husbands."

"Let's hope so."

"Hey," he said, suddenly. "I've seen your show a few times. Pretty good. Very tasteful. They keep the sex discreet. I like that."

The Deer

I had gone into town for a cup of green tea and was just returning.

There was an immediate problem at home when I arrived.

In fact, there seemed to always be some sort of issue with that blasphemed pool.

What now?

Tony ran up to me in a panic.

"Come quick."

We scaled the stairs and made our way to the roof. I looked across the pool and saw something swimming in it.

"Who is that?" I asked, not really seeing what it was.

"It's a deer."

The deer swam around the pool looking scared and helpless. It tried to jump up on the side but couldn't quite gain footing with its slick hooves.

"What should we do?" asked Tony.

The poor deer was frightened and kept cutting itself in the neck as her hooves scratched her. It grunted and squeaked.

"How did a deer get in here, Tony?"

"It's a long story."

"What happened?" I asked, assessing what I should do.

Tony explained to me that the son had seen the deer in the front yard.

He wanted to grab his camera to take a photo and ran upstairs, leaving open the front door. Apparently the deer entered, went up the stairs, and made its way out to the roof.

"That's what we figured, at least."

The father suddenly appeared with his camera. "Tony, where's your camera?"

"It's downstairs, sir."

"Go get it, man!"

"I need him to help me," I insisted.

"Okay, fine, yeah, whatever, do it, now, go, save the deer. This will be great."

He pointed the camera about two inches from my face.

"Where's my son?"

"He's drinking in his room," Tony replied.

"Figures."

I can only describe the next scene as excruciating.

We had called the fire department, but they must have thought it was a prank call because no one from there came.

I couldn't watch the deer flounder around anymore and decided on a plan.

Since I refused to enter the water, I needed Tony to dive in for me, but even if he did, he could do very little.

The deer was now bleeding from its neck from the hoof lacerations.

Blood filled the pool and I didn't know what to do.

I had no viable idea and it looked like the deer might bleed to death. After it made many attempts to ascend the side, it gave up and swam to the middle of the pool. I watched its eyes close and then it sank to the bottom. Tony began crying and I bit my lip.

A helicopter had to airlift the body out the next morning, and I will never forget the sight of the stiff deer in a harness as the uproar of the helicopter echoed throughout North Street.

I Begin to Drink Copiously

A depression came over me after seeing the deer die.

My worst fears had supervened and I was lost.

I checked into the Howard Johnson's on the Post Road and put a "Do Not Disturb" sign on my doorknob.

I just wanted quiet and no cameras and no women and to be pure again somehow.

There was little escape.

I began to go to the local bar and drink gin.

Every night I ended up across the border in Port Chester at one of the New York bars that stay open until four a.m.

I went home with random nannies, hairdressers, and divorcees.

I never learned last names and we were mutually disposable to one another.

One night, I was by myself. A milquetoast of a man came right up to me while I was sitting at the bar.

"I know what you did to my wife. She's pregnant now."

"I'm sorry," I mumbled, nearly seeing double from all the gin and tonics.

My vision was a blur and I couldn't remember his face.

"No, I want to thank you. We couldn't get pregnant on our own. I just wanted offer my appreciation."

"You're welcome," I said, glad that there would be no knife involved.

A bachelorette party barged into the establishment like cattle coming home for hay and they were as inebriated as I was. Two pretty girls seemed to recognize me from television and they continued to buy me all sorts of shots: SoCo and Lime, Lemon Drops, Kamikazes, Red Snappers, Jäger Bombs, Goldschläger. I didn't care. I poured them into my mouth as if they were water.

I left with the two girls, one of whom was to be married in a matter of weeks.

We came back to a house in Greenwich and there were snowdrifts of cocaine in the kitchen.

I scooped it up my nostrils like cereal and then I witnessed what I never thought I would.

I was making love to two girls but feeling like hell.

It was difficult bliss.

They backed away from me and proceeded to get into a fistfight, laughing the whole time.

They were naked and punching each other hard in the face.

They traded licks in this manner and I found myself newly aroused by this odd feminine pugilism.

"Harder!" one yelled, after being socked.

"Even harder!" the other yelled, after receiving a quite a right hook.

Then in the middle of it I puked up all of my guts, all of everything.

So much came out of me, rivers of vomit, lakes of bile.

I was only able to be with women for short periods of time and I knew no last names.

Where were my clothes?

I didn't care.

I left the house with the two girls fighting each other in their living room.

"A tooth," one screamed, giddily. "You knocked out a tooth! All right!"

The last thing I saw was the two of them hugging each other.

I walked down Greenwich Avenue with no clothes and the walk turned into a sprint. My mouth was so dry that I felt like I had eaten hot sand.

I wanted to suddenly be someone else.

I ran all the way to the water where the ferry boats leave and it was dark as coal.

The moon was like a white button on the summer linen shirt of God and I fell onto a bench, put my head in my hands, and prayed to somehow wake up in a different way.

It was then that I was blinded by my profuse hubris. I tried to consider what oblation I could offer beyond bread and wine, what sacrifice I could make to change in some way.

I was at my low point: naked on a bench in Greenwich, disgusted with myself.

I began to cry and wish for my clothes.

I was a drunk and sleeping late right through the mornings, turning into a nocturnal person who wanted nothing to do with daylight.

Afraid of people. My eyes became so sensitive to light that I couldn't even go outside until six in the evening.

I was no longer the matutinal pool cleaner listening to birds as I bettered the existence of a pool.

My chlorinated soul was turning into detritus and was a sad version of its former self.

What I mostly missed was the past, the Eden of my childhood where everything I did was right.

I missed Linda Rabeson.

Finally, I managed to walk to the train station where a cabbie took me to the mansion on North Street.

I stumbled through the house, up the stairs, and to the pool where I sat and listened to the water for hours until the sun rose.

After Contemplation, I Decide to Form my Own Religion

That very morning, I made calls to all of my former paramours and invited them to the house.

So many women came that I realized what a need there was for such a new belief.

It had been right in front of me the whole time: Pool.

The mother was not so happy about the house metamorphosing into a church overnight.

"You can't do this to our home," the mother said.

"Why not?"

"It's our house."

"It is a House of Pool now."

"House of Pool?"

"Amen," I said.

"Amen?"

"So be it."

She rolled her eyes.

"You're a damn hypocrite and you and I need to have a little conversation about this kid I'm having."

"In time, my child. In time."

"What is wrong with you? Did you get hit on the head?"

"I am fine."

My congregation consisted of women that were forty-two years and older.

They all worshiped me with ardor and completeness.

I made it clear to them that I was no God and that to think of me as such was to violate one of the most potent commandments to humankind.

I merely wanted them to see that their pools were living spirits, secret words from the Deity that reminded us of the lucid sweetness of water's essence.

I stopped having sex with everyone and suggested that they all do the same.

They followed in me in this manner for many months.

Ironically, the pool at the house became filthy during this time.

It was as if it had been cursed by the dead deer.

Tony wouldn't help out anymore either.

To be honest, I was a little afraid of it myself.

There was no balance. Algae filled up the clear blue water with a slimy green color.

Nevertheless, after the house became our first church, all the other houses on North Street began to follow suit and open up their doors as churches.

The Church of Pool now had over 2,000 female members and I was their leader.

The father, however, was not too happy with me. He had tried to film the growth of the church but nobody wanted to see a church reality show. "Pool Man" was canceled on television. The son fared much better, though, because he followed us along for months and his documentary detailed the religious conversions of several billionaire women who began speaking in tongues. Their moments of sublime glossolalia contained so much verisimilitude that the son's film not only went to Sundance and Cannes, but actually won an Oscar for Best Documentary.

It was at the Oscars where I met Ron Howard who happened to live in Greenwich.

Isn't that always the case: you can live in the same town as a famous director, but you have to go to the Oscars to get his phone number.

He gave me his card and told me to call him. Do not make any Opie or Richie jokes around him. He indicated that a cult had forced him to perform those particular television roles.

Our church was a practical one as well.

We often had experts give tips on things like adding preemptive blister pads to your sandals or making your own age-correcting facial serum at home.

Somehow, the church became a haven for women only.

The son, too, had transformed after his Oscar win.

Time was only a thought then and suddenly the mother and the daughter-in-law were having their children.

In fact, many of the women in the congregation began to have babies around the same time as well, some even on the same day.

No one seemed to care or acknowledge that most of the children were mine, maybe all of them.

I had to do something.

Here were my sins returning to me.

Or were they?

Maybe this was a chance to truly alter the path of corruption I had seen all my life.

We were all wanting to go back to innocence, to never fall again.

Here was a pool of innocents.

I had to do the right thing but what was that?

I took to wearing chlorine blue robes. My sermons never occurred in the mornings because I liked to sleep late.

"Ladies," I usually began. "Thank you for coming again to honor Pool. Pool is a state of mind, a place of peace. You have made the decision to let go of carnal pleasures and to exist in the realm of intense contemplation. For this, you shall be rewarded with a stillness of heart. Many of you have been having my children, all weirdly enough, in the same week. I want to congratulate you while also apologizing for interfering in your bad marriages. These children are now symbols of change. I will help you raise them."

Many of the women cheered.

Ron Howard came by later and talked to me about co-writing a screenplay.

It was to be about a talking pool, a story for children but one that also existed in the mature realm of adult metonymy. The pool would come under the attack of a mean matron who would view it only as a place for people to swim and do drugs, but Pool Man (played by me) would come along and fight this antagonist to the death.

I had abstained from sex completely and stopped drinking altogether.

My life felt fresh, no longer fuzzy.

One night, Rose sneaked into my room.

"Well," she said, her arms folded with our child.

"Um, what's its name?"

"It?"

"Her?"

"Try his."

"His. What's his name?"

It was a beautiful child and he looked just like me.

"Gneiss."

"Is that his name or a euphemism for his ca-ca?"

"You don't like it?" she pleaded, desperately concerned.

"Um, what does Gneiss mean?"

"It's a metamorphic rock with many different layers."

"Ah. And why did you pick this name in particular?"

"It's a family name."

"I see."

"Look, I am leaving my husband."

"But . . . he just won an Oscar."

"So. We never have sex anymore after the baby was born."

"Did you ever before?"

"No," she admitted. "And you're all celibate now. Useless."

"I'm sorry but I am only devoted to Pool now."

"You and that damn pool. It's in the worst shape ever."

She put down the boy.

I touched her face and arousal shot through me as if I had been injected in the arm with it.

I Sin

But I began a litany of coitus with my entire congregation. What began as a pristine garden turned quickly into a debauched house of narcissistic iniquity.

Most of the women were stimulated immediately because of their postpartum insecurities about their bodies, but I had never cared about bodily flaws.

They were merely foreplay for me.

Things turned into a mess.

I was now a hypocrite vacillating between a pure place and an impure one.

It seemed like I had confused and irritated a lot of people.

My show was no longer a hit.

Ron Howard backed off the screenplay. I began to see babies all over Greenwich that looked like me. It was a nightmare. The religion of Pool now seemed duplicitous to me.

I was drinking gin alone again at the bar. Out of the blue, Rose appeared. She was right in my face. I was in another fog of alcohol, almost stumbling over myself. I had to pee badly.

"How did you get here?"

I could barely keep open my eyes.

"Shh. You have to come with me."

"Why?"

"My husband is livid. He just found out about the baby. I told him."

"I thought he didn't care."

We ducked back into the bar and she dragged me to the back patio. "You are in serious trouble."

"What should I do?"

"Do not go back to the house?"

"Why?"

"He's gone a little nuts."

"What do you mean?"

"Just stay away from the house, okay?"

"I can't. I need to go back."

"Be careful then. He's waiting for you."

A Catastrophe Turns Slowly into a Dream

There was no sign of the son, but an emergency had occurred. Things had gotten really out of hand. Manku ran up to me and yelled, "Dee dee dee."

I thought he meant his teeth because he had plats (jewelry) in his front two molars. He wore a motorcycle helmet and an orange life vest.

Tony was right behind him in his Speedo. "We have a serious problem."

"What's the matter?" I responded. "You eat a bad steroid or something?"

"You're hilarious," he said, without smiling. "Come quick, I'll show you."

We scaled all the stairs to the roof and walked outside to the pool. It was half-empty. "There's a leak somewhere!" Tony screamed.

"Calm down."

"Do you know how long it takes to fill up that damn thing?"

"It'll be fine."

"Last time this happened, we drained the Greenwich reservoir."

There was a dreamy mist over the water.

It was stupefying.

Nothing like this calamity had ever happened under my watch, and you could even see the water draining.

There was a massive hole and I could just make it out in the bottom corner on the other side.

Not one to ever lose my equanimity, I thought quickly then redoubled my attempt to find a quick solution.

I saw the ladder, which went all the way to the bottom, but I could see the hole and it was on the other side of the ladder. I needed to dive and get to the hole quickly, and the ladder would take me too long.

Without thinking anymore (because thought is the death knell to action), I stripped my clothes and got a running start and dove from the edge and flew thirty feet through the air.

It was a marvelous moment of honor to the pool because implicit in my derring-do was a soothing trust for the water that would always protect me.

When I splashed, I realized that it was the first time that I had ever entered the pool.

The warmth of the water embraced me and I realized that even though I was not a good swimmer that inside the pool was like the womb for me.

It was familiar and almost made me want to sever my social umbilical cord.

I opened my eyes, not worried about the chlorine damaging them.

I was more concerned with how the chlorine might affect my new hair tints.

Then I saw the hole.

It was a crack in the pool at the bottom corner. All of that concrete was bound to go at some point. I was losing breath but wanted to examine the hole up close. I fought the water as I swam down more. There was still thirty feet of water.

When I stood on the bottom and saw the hole, I panicked. A fissure ran all the way to the top and its cleavage was widening. I swam as quickly as I could to the surface, barely able to breathe.

Once I reached the top, I then had to climb the ladder the rest of the way, another thirty feet.

My lungs raged for oxygen and I mounted the rungs of the ladder as fast as I could.

Tony and Manku waited for me with apprehension.

"Well?" Tony said.

"Get away from the pool as fast as you can."

"Why? What's wrong?"

I wiped water from my eyes.

"Run to the roof! Now!

We all sprinted from the side of the pool and made our way onto the roof.

"Tony, run downstairs and call the fire department."

"Why?"

"Just call them!"

I told Manku to remain with me and as we watched, the sides of the pool began calving and splintering like a glacier.

The white painted concrete avalanched into the water like people from a sinking ship.

The splashes went as high as the roof and all four sides were caving and creating a thick soup of rock and water. The pool was closely attached to the house and by glass in places, and I realized that I needed to warn everyone.

I saw the thick glass cracking.

I ran into the house and yelled at everyone to evacuate as soon as possible.

I pushed out the maid and all of the family. We ran into the small front yard and something happened that I will never forget.

The remaining water in the pool had no outlet except the small hole.

True, the pool was only half its size but it was still millions of gallons.

The glass had broken in the wall and the water was coming into the house!

As we watched from the yard, the bottom windows filled up first and they busted open cracking.

Water poured into the yard and we now backed into the street and stopped cars on North Street.

All that water was rushing out of the house and drowning the yard and washing away the road.

It was a nightmare for a Pool Man like me.

When I looked up at the bright sky, I saw the barrel of a pistol about ten feet away and the shot came at me after a cacophony of gun powder exploding. I felt like I saw the bullet. The son had pulled the trigger and the bullet dug right into my face like fire that had been inserted under my skin. He dropped the gun and ran. I crawled over to the hot piece and grabbed it.

The father was out there with his camera filming the whole thing.

"Holy shit," he yelled. "You shot him. Wow, that'll come out great."

"I think I'm bleeding," I said.

He pointed the camera at my face and zoomed in as close as he could.

I saw the lens come at me like a train in a 3-D movie.

"Just let me get this shot. Whoa, you are gushing, man. I can't believe this. I've always thought my son should be in prison and now I have it all on tape."

"Get that camera out of my face. Please."

I smelled the warm blood as it covered my lips and oozed into my mouth and covered my tongue.

"I will. One last shot. You want to pretend to die or something? That could be cool."

"Well, I think I am dying."

"Yeah, you might be right. That bullet could be up in your brain somewhere. Let me call 911."

"How about this for one last shot!!!" I Bruce-Willised, lifting the gun, aiming, and shooting the camera four times. It fell to the asphalt with a crash and cracked into pieces.

"Why'd you do that?" he pleaded, trying to see if he could salvage the tape.

He couldn't.

It was Mengta (whom I had met on the first day and only walked by her and issued perfunctory hellos thereafter): she was the one to hold my bleeding head cupped in her hands.

"You're a good Pool Man," she said. "This is not your fault."

And my eyes closed.

A Change of Face

The knife was a sublime incision under my mandible. The bullet had forced me under the scalpel of one of the top plastic surgeons in Connecticut. I'm not sure how they measure who actually wins this contest, but all the nurses assured me that Dr. Lhotse from Nepal was at the top of his game.

"He did all twelve of Zsa Zsa Gabor's facelifts," one said.

"He did her cat too."

This was a beautiful world, I thought, where actresses could get facelifts and so could cats.

It mesmerized me away from the pain to think these thoughts.

Rhytidectomy had ever been a goal of mine, and now it was happening.

When I refused anesthesia, the whole group couldn't understand why I would want to do such a thing.

The blood had been stanched at this point and I could talk a little. It was here that I explained to them how I had wanted a facelift since I was a child. When I was younger, it made no sense to get one, though, and I had saved the experience as a dream, a dream I would honor at the right moment.

I said that I hoped the bullet would not affect my ability to have the operation that I wanted for *me*. Yes, it was selfish, but it was my choice and I needed to be as perspicuous as possible in giving them my reasons.

To be unclear about my goals would utterly subvert the only perfect vision I had ever had for myself.

"You see," I continued, as they all stared kindly at me on the operating table under the bright white and silver lights. It's important for me to stay awake and see everything that you do."

"I don't think we can legally do that," Dr. Lhotse said.

"Why not?" I pleaded.

"Well, I just—" he continued but was interrupted.

"Hey, weren't you on that t.v. show?" the head nurse said, suddenly recognizing me.

I said that I was. She covered her mouth in gleeful surprise, as the other two nurses tittered with her like little mice that have just discovered some free cheese.

"You look just like him!" the head nurse said.

"Well . . . I am him!" I reminded her.

"Um," the doctor spoke. "Can we try to get this going? We need to dig out the bullet from under your eye."

"That sounds like it might hurt," I said.

"Oh it will. A lot."

"I don't mind the pain," I let him know.

I don't know if you've ever been shot in the face at close range, but it's pretty dangerous.

The vengeful son had just missed hitting my eye by about an inch.

The doctor agreed to forgo the ether.

There I was, wide wake as he slid a knife under my skin and rooted around for the bullet.

"Somehow," he explained while he worked, "your cheekbone absorbed most of the bullet. So the only damage you might have is localized."

"That's good," I said, grimacing from the most excruciating pain I had ever felt in my life.

It was a bully jumping up and down on a pogo stick right on my stomach.

Like a pig digging for truffles, the knife finally succeeded in rescuing the bullet from the blood muck.

Nurse Person held my hand and I had to say that even in the moment of trauma, I was aroused by her age.

"You're a lovely one," I said to her. Although I was in serious pain, I continued to be affable and endearing.

"Thank you," she responded, blushing. For a moment, my mind diverted to her zaftig beauty. I visualized her touching herself to my television show.

The next six hours involved slicing my face right at the hairline.

"Oh," I just remembered. "Can you make sure to get rid of some those fat deposits—in addition to face tightening?"

"Sure," said the doctor. "That's standard anyway for this kind of operation."

"Oh good." I was quite relieved. "And one more thing."

"What's that?"

"I have a picture I want you to use, the sort of face I want."

"Where is it?"

"It's in the back pocket of my jeans."

"Nurse, go find his jeans."

Nurse Person left and returned with the photograph and handed it to the doctor.

He raised his eyebrows and shook his head. "You sure about this?"

"I am."

I floated in and out of awareness.

I was able to see the operation on a television since I had a camera pointed at me.

During one of my moments of sleep, I had a vision of a hidden road covered with ice.

I walked this road and saw no one else but Linda Rabeson coming toward me.

She was minute, but I knew it was she by her posture. I could recognize her from any distance. Suddenly, there were deer everywhere and they all had wings the color of cream. None of them was flying and they seemed to protect me as I walked.

The sky cleared and Linda was nowhere to be found and then some sort of entity with three heads approached me.

One head was my face, one was my new face, and one was the head of Linda.

They were all pointed away from each other and their mouths moved at the same time.

The day became hotter and the ice melted quickly. As the ice poured around my feet, my sweat commingled within it—and a pool began to form with invisible walls. The ice water and sweat filled up ten feet and then rose higher. It was as if the shape of the pool was a rectangle but there were no walls containing it.

And yet it was self-contained and rising higher and higher on up into the sky. I floated on the top the entire way. As I approached the sun, I opened a door and entered that bright orb. Inside, was Funny Duck welcoming me.

I wondered about Linda Rabeson but before I was able to visualize her anywhere, before I could make sense of why I had risen so high and disappeared into the sun, before I could wonder anymore about the three-headed person, I woke up as a knife slid under my skin, like some sort of endless paper cut and I screamed for the first time in my life. I screamed out all the impurities I had created and I forgave myself for those I had hurt without intention.

There was no pain and I waited eagerly for the final result.

15 Years Later

There's not much to tell now.

I continued to live in Greenwich for many years and became more of a pool consultant.

It started to get a little uncomfortable around town when I would see ten to fifteen kids every day that looked exactly like me.

Well, the old me.

My new face disguised me better than I could have imagined. In fact, no one recognized me at all.

I wanted to put my television years behind me.

I even decided to raise one of the many kids I had fathered, partially as a favor to the last family for whom I worked.

Before there could even be a trial, the documentary filmmaker son apparently lost his mind, filled the crumbled pool structure with several hundred gallons of ketchup, and jumped from the roof to his death.

I ended up raising his son, who was actually my son anyway from the daughter-in-law.

She and I share him in an amicable way. The mother had her baby too and that child calls me Uncle Pool now.

As the years passed, I couldn't convince my son to go into pooling.

He began his own landscaping business and decided to become Lawn Boy, to my dismay really.

Lawning is just plain loud and violent with all those noise

machines they use to blow the leaves from one side of the yard to the other.

I remember when Lawn Boy was recovering from rubella at the age of twelve and he came to me with a bunch of questions.

"Dad, why do you have so many kids, but I'm the only one you decided to raise?"

"It's a long story, Lawn Boy."

"When will I be Lawn Man?"

"In time, son."

"I want to be Lawn Man now. I hate the German Measles."

"You have to be patient."

"But I don't like spending time with older women after I mow the lawn."

"You don't have to do anything you don't want to do."

"They make me drink cola with them and they stare at me."

"They like you then, don't they?"

"But I'm not you, Dad. I don't want that life. I'm ashamed of what you did."

"Now, wait a second. If you're referring to all the women that I loved—"

"You didn't love them."

"Maybe not. But I cared for them and we took care of each other."

I thought of Linda Rabeson at that moment and decided to call her some day to say hello. I had taken a vow of chastity and decided to never have gratuitous sex again.

"Don't be so hard on your formerly orphaned father."

"It's just that I get teased a lot because of you."

"I'm sorry for that. I've tried to be a good dad to you."

"You have. Yes. But what about all of your other kids?"

"I know," I said with shame. "I'm not perfect."

He ignored me for a few days and it sent me into reflection about what was right.

But during that time, I finally located Linda's number and called her. I didn't even know if she would be alive. She was in her eighties.

"Hello?" I said, very nervously.

"Is that you?" she asked. She knew my voice and I knew hers.

"Yes," I said. "It is."

"I have missed you very much," she said.

"I have missed you too, Linda."

There was a silence on the phone for a moment and I imagined her again, all those times in her bed where we touched but nothing else.

It was a pure time that I suddenly missed more than anything.

She lived by herself at this point and I asked if she would like to come to Greenwich. She booked a ticket and I picked her up at JFK two days later.

When I saw her at the airport, the same warmth was there. And when we looked at each other and hugged, it filled us both.

I thought of my vision of her years earlier while I was under the knife.

"You look so different," she said.

"Do you like it?"

"I had heard about you being shot. I was worried."

"So do you like the facelift?"

She grabbed my chin with her hand and turned me from side to side.

"I love it," she said. "Of course."

At home I introduced her to my son.

"This is Lawn Boy," I said.

"Hi," she said, beaming.

"Hello," he said, smiling.

They liked each other from the beginning and she turned my house into something beyond love.

She was the only reality I had ever known.

Every once in awhile, I would become dejected about all the years I could have been with her.

The shame of my earlier life would consume me and I thought I had maybe squandered the most important time of my youth.

"No," she said, touching my face. "That's not true."

"And this facelift . . . isn't it shallow?"

"Not at all," she assured me.

"I feel I have not lived the best way that I could have."

"You've been with me all along," she said, softly.

It was this kind of support that allowed me to gain the confidence to run for the Connecticut Senate.

I won with her help, even though we ran into a media avalanche when they discovered that my very own son was not a pool boy but lawn-oriented.

My opponent ran ads in which the screen was split.

I was cleaning a pool on one side, while Lawn Boy destroyed something with a weed whacker on the other side.

"This hypocrite," the mudslinging voiceover began, "lost his own son to the lawn business. Why?"

They also brought up my past.

Several women I had known were interviewed on E! saying that I was the worst sort of roué and not any sort of family man to lead the state.

I maintained my equanimity throughout the process and was given a final voting boost when it was discovered that my opponent had dated Michael Jackson at some point.

During my last appearance on "Letterman," Dave asked me about my facelift, of course.

"You look like a woman," he remarked.

"I know," I said.

"You *wanted* to look like a woman?"

"Yes."

"But why?"

I shrugged. "My reasons."

The audience chuckled.

"Okay," he said, smiling. "I understand too that you have a new CD?"

"Yes, that's right."

"Pool Man. Senator. Musician. Where do you find the time?"

"Well, this CD is not exactly my music."

He held it up to the camera for a close-up. "*Songs from Under the Pool* is the title."

"That's right."

"And what is it? I tried to listen to it before the show, but it sounded like a bunch of gurgling."

"Just sounds of pools that I've collected over the years."

"All right," he said. "Now let's get to the real story here . . ."

I had hoped that he would concentrate more on my politics, but he seemed to be more intrigued by my past.

I sighed and told him that I had behaved that way because of emptiness.

"I can't speak in regret because a true Pool Man serves a purpose. And for me to negate that aspect of my own history would be a senseless denial. Someone once asked me if it was empty, what I did. Empty? No, not at all. Just busy. I was always really busy. My advice: pick one pool and stay there, but swim in many before you do."

One of the first laws that I enacted as senator was the "Urine-Free Pool Act." It passed in large measure due to my door-to-door campaign where I agreed to clean every pool in Connecticut. I honored my offer and also gained a world record as well.

Linda was my gun moll, my Pool Woman.

There are not a lot of Pool Women around and I am quite certain that she was the best one that I had known.

Linda died about ten years after I ended my Senate tenure. At the funeral I remember my son trying to hide his weeping. He loved her just as I had, as a lovely, lovely, lovely lady, a paragon of all the ladies there are.

Epilogue

After Linda died and Lawn Boy went off to the Lawn College of Staten Island, I was alone all the time and made a decision to offer myself as a legacy.

With the help of Funny Duck, I was frozen in a form-fitting capsule and placed in the Pool Museum of San Diego where I still reside today.

It is free admission.

For a while, I was alive and could talk to you, but I am dead now.

With the help of this recorder, though, you can continue to hear my story.

One thing you might notice is that my face is the face of Linda Rabeson. When we were together, it turned some heads for sure. I had always wanted to look like her.

If you have a hard time finding me, I am sandwiched in an alcove between the seals and the orcas.

If you ever decide to build your own pool, I do make the suggestion that you hire a pool boy. There are quite a few of them who have been trained by me and they have my imprimatur.

Don't try to clean the pool on your own because you will mess it up. It is an artist's craft and should not be taken lightly.

In fact, at current count, there are only eleven true Pool Men remaining and their attenuated numbers have given rise to several political action committees.

If you want to donate, please call: 1 800 POOL MAN.

Believe it or not, Funny Duck is still alive and he continues to provide his services for the cause.

■ ■ ■

I leave you with a few thoughts that I have considered over the years:

The pool is a quiet being with a life of its own.

It murmurs the most simplistic humming to remind us that we must enjoy ourselves, but there is also a soft historical resonance that is more serious.

In fencing, a pool is a match during which the members of one team, one after another, plays against the members of the opposing team.

This definition may not seem significant, but it is just another example of how much meaning a pool contains.

Pool is infinite.

Pool is a verity not defined.

It is relevant and tangential.

It needs to stay clean.

And if you listen very closely, you hear its slow breaths at night.

CPSIA information can be obtained at www.ICGtesting.com
Printed in the USA
LVOW090059020612

284004LV00005B/1/P